ALSO BY LEIA STONE

WOLF GIRL
Wolf Girl
Lost Girl
Alpha Girl
Mated Girl

GILDED CITY
House of Ash and Shadow
House of War and Bone
House of Light and Ether

KINGS OF AVALIER
The Last Dragon King
The Broken Elf King
The Ruthless Fae King
The Forbidden Wolf King

FALLEN ACADEMY
Fallen Academy: Year One
Fallen Academy: Year Two
Fallen Academy: Year Three
Fallen Academy: Year Four

ALPHA GIRL

LEIA STONE

Bloom books

Published by Bloom Books, an imprint of Sourcebooks
P.O. Box 4410, Naperville, Illinois 60567–4410
(630) 961-3900
sourcebooks.com

Originally self-published in 2021 by Leia Stone LLC.

Cataloging-in-Publication data is on file with the Library of Congress.

Printed and bound in the United States of America.
KP 10 9 8 7 6 5 4 3 2 1

For my family.

CHAPTER ONE

SAGE AND I BURST THROUGH THE FOREST AS WE RAN blindly, away from the haunting howl of Sawyer's voice. I felt him shut down inside of our bond.

He went completely numb and it killed me.

'I'll be right back,' I kept saying over and over, mostly to assuage my own guilt.

He stopped responding, but I knew he had a war to deal with.

"We need to be careful not to step into Ithaki land," I told Sage as I leaped over a fallen log. There was a visible line on the ground made of crushed blue stones, and I hoped we were on the right side of it. I was running away from Waterfall Mountain, which I knew to be Ithaki land, and toward the direction Astra had run when we'd said goodbye.

Sage was in wolf form behind me, but I was running

as a human. For now. My wolf was begging to come out, but I still wasn't sure if that was a good idea. I wanted to have a good first impression with the Paladin people, and I didn't want to roll up to their homelands and be like, *Yo, I'm your alpha and I need ten thousand men, and I'm also a split shifter. Everything is fine, nothing to see here.*

Wolf Angel is what Arrow had called what I was.

Maybe they would be cool with it…me, my powers, the fact that I was about to ask a very big favor…

'Alpha?' Astra's voice suddenly boomed in my mind and I stopped dead, catching my breath. I didn't want to run too fast and lose Sage, so I wasn't using my super speed powers.

'Astra! Where are you?' I spun around, scanning the dark forest. I felt her. It was hard to explain, but I knew she was near. My body thrummed with power the deeper we stepped into this land.

Pack, my wolf chanted, excited at the prospect of seeing Astra. I'd sort of mentally glossed over the fact that I'd bitten her and claimed her as my pack member. But now I was completely confronted with it.

'Alpha! You came home!' Her jubilation spread through my limbs until a bubble of laughter burst from my chest. Sage gave me an incredulous look as I ran in the direction that I felt Astra.

'I need to speak to you, and Arrow and…everyone,' I told her.

My wolf was beyond excited to be here, but I was tempering that excitement and focusing on the goal.

I needed a couple thousand warriors by morning. I'd promised Sawyer and I *would* come through.

"Alpha!" Astra's excited scream ripped through the dark night as Sage and I altered course to follow the noise.

Suddenly twigs snapped all around us in a circle, and floodlights turned on. We both froze. Astra burst from the trees, grinning just as over a dozen warriors, all naked but for a suede junk cover, stepped out with bows and arrows, spears, and knives. Rich blue paint streaked down their cheeks in thin lines, and they looked absolutely one hundred percent ready to kill us both.

Sage's head snapped to me and I swallowed hard.

"Alpha!" Astra threw herself in my arms as I embraced her, wrapping my arms around her thin form and ignoring the twelve angry men glaring at me. The earth vibrated under my feet and my wolf pounded against my chest, begging to be freed.

"She came!" Astra pulled away, pushing her brown hair from her face as she grinned at the armed men. "Praise the Father, she came like I said she would!"

The men didn't lower their weapons; they simply glared at me with disdain, nostrils flaring. "City wolf," one of them growled. "Go back home. You're not welcome here."

I cleared my throat nervously. "Actually, if I could speak to Arrow—"

"Go home." Arrow stepped out from behind the line of men and the hurt in his voice caused a frown to pull at my lips. "We don't want any more of your *charity.*"

So that's what this was about. I saved their lives with food and they were acting like dicks over it? Astra spun, crossing her arms over her chest as if they'd pierced her with their nasty words. "What's the matter with you?" she shouted, her voice shaking. "This is our alpha! She's come to save us. She'll heal the land *and* our people."

I swallowed hard as Sage's gaze flicked to mine, wide-eyed.

One of the men, holding a knife, lowered it to his side and stepped out from the trees, deeper into the flood-lights. Pale light and shadows danced across his perfectly toned body as I met his hardened gaze. He looked about twenty-five years old, and had a scar running from the bottom of his eye to his lip.

"Is that right? Are you here to save us like my brother and Astra say?" He tipped his head to Arrow, who promptly looked down at his feet. "Or are you just a witch who has tricked everyone?"

I recoiled at his accusation. I wasn't expecting this frosty reception. "I...I'm not a witch. I came because I need help. The city wolves are at war, and obviously I'll help you in return, if—"

Every single warrior burst into laughter then, and I heard even more voices, men and women, from deeper in the tree line behind the bright lights.

Fuck.

The floodlights had tiny solar panels on top of them, and when I let my eyes adjust I noticed the shadowy figures in the trees looking down on us. Hundreds of people listened on.

"You want our help because your *stupid alpha* started a war?" He spat at my feet and I felt the wetness brush across the front of my legs. "You're not my alpha." The scar-faced man growled and everyone cheered in response, all of them. Their laughs and yells of agreement rang into my soul, twisting into me like a hot knife.

Unbridled rage ripped through me at his disrespect toward me and to Sawyer, and I couldn't hold my wolf in any longer. She burst from my chest. One second she was a ghost and the next she solidified, hitting the scar-faced dude in the chest, knocking him on his ass and making him drop his knife.

Gasps rang throughout the forest as my wolf peeled her lips back, saliva glistening on her teeth as she eyed his throat. I knelt beside her on the forest floor as dozens of Paladin warriors stepped close. I stared Scar Face down as he looked up at me with wide blue eyes.

"I *am* daughter of Running Spirit, granddaughter of Red Moon, and if you *ever* spit on me again, I'll rip your balls out with my teeth," I growled.

A chorus of female whoops and cheers ran throughout the forest, but the men stayed silent. I was well aware of the challenge I'd issued, but I wasn't going to let this prick ruin everything. Pelts of fur ran down the man's face as his wolf started to emerge. A firm hand fell on my shoulder, and then I was yanked backward, my wolf retreating with me.

I spun to see who'd pulled me off, thinking it was Sage, only to see Arrow's piercing blue eyes.

"We have dominance fights that end in death. I would take it easy until you learn the rules here," Arrow whispered in my ear.

Oh.

People sometimes got in fistfights for dominance in Wolf City, but it wasn't like a *real* dominance fight you heard about hundreds of years ago. Was I ready to get in some fight right now and kill this guy to prove to them I was an alpha? I just came here for help. I *needed* help.

"But I'm…" I couldn't even say it now. It felt wrong. Was I an alpha? Astra and Arrow had begged for my help and I'd merely sent them food. *Oh God.* Guilt and shame burned its way across my skin until my entire face felt hot.

"The title of alpha needs to be earned," Arrow murmured under his breath, as his brother fought his wolf's change. "You've earned a bit of respect with the women just now, but the men won't be so easy. Your charity food delivery, instead of coming to meet everyone, was a poor choice."

Shit.

I opened my mouth to speak, but the man who I'd just knocked on his ass stood and glared at Arrow.

"Can she stay, Rab?" Arrow asked. "Prove herself? Enter the alpha trial?"

Alpha what now? Stay and prove myself? Fuck that, we were at war.

"No. I need your help," I pleaded. "I can't stay. The witches, fey, vampires, they are all together now. They are marching on Wolf City as we speak. I need warriors or thousands will die. Please."

Rab, or whatever his name was, gave me a maniacal grin, the thick scar pressing his lip down in a lopsided sneer. He stepped closer to me, slowly. My wolf gave a low warning growl and he stopped.

"*You* need warriors?" he asked, and I couldn't get a read on him. "You need *our* help or *your* people will die?"

I nodded. "As many as you can spare. And in exchange I'll send more food, monthly even—"

"You need warriors… Okay, then, we can send you some weapons." His grin widened and the men cheered and clapped their hands.

I frowned. Confused. Weapons. Like spears and arrows? No thanks.

"I don't need weapons, I need—"

He growled in my face and I froze. "We didn't need *food*! We need our land healed. We need our pack's power restored, our crops replenished. You put a Band-Aid on a bullet hole and now you expect us to help *you*?"

He laughed, tipping his head back, and the men in the darkness of the trees joined him.

Fuck.

He met my gaze and his eyes flashed golden yellow. "I'd rather turn into a human and starve to death than follow a cowardice *alpha* like you."

He spun then, giving me his back, and walked away.

Each one of his words lashed into me, cutting deep into the bone, into the very core of who I was. I'd rejected Arrow's plea for help to restore their people and their land, and then I'd come and asked for the same thing.

My body sagged with shame. Arrow had told me thousands would die and I needed to return home to help them, and I'd sent dried food and fucking firewood. This was a moment of reckoning, one that would haunt me for the rest of my life if I didn't choose wisely.

"You're right!" I yelled, and Rab froze.

An eerie calm washed over the space as a chilly wind rose into the air, whipping my hair around my face.

"When Arrow and Astra told me they needed my help, I panicked. I don't know your ways, I only just learned who my real father was, and my life has been hard enough. I was selfish. I wanted to get married and live an easy life and not have to worry about other people's problems." My lower lip quivered with the truth and it felt dirty in my mouth. I wanted to spit it out.

Boos came from the trees, but they were soft, accepting and admonishing at the same time.

I lowered my head, thinking of Astra and Arrow's heartfelt pleas.

Our people are dying.
The land is dying.
Our magic is dying.
Come home.

I'd just...ignored him. My throat constricted with emotion and I cleared it, steadying myself. "I've come home," I declared, the goosebumps on my arms standing up as the wind rushed past me faster. "I've come home to save our people *and* our land, if you will forgive me and give me a chance. Let me prove I'm worthy to hold the title of alpha."

Rab spun as the people in the trees started to beat on the trunks with their fists, cheering as they screamed into the night. It was fierce and beautiful, and my wolf tipped her head back and howled at the moon right along with them. This felt right, this was where I belonged, where I was needed, but as soon as I thought it, Sawyer's pained wail sifted across my memory and I swallowed hard.

I needed to be alpha. I couldn't let these people down, my people. I needed to do both. Be both a Paladin and a city wolf.

"Send the warriors I need by first light and I *will* stay. I will stay here as long as needed and do whatever is required of me to save this land and these people." I gestured to the trees and the howls and cheers got louder in agreement. More of them must have come, because it

9

sounded like a chorus of thousands all echoing into the treetops.

Rab watched me with two thin blue eyes, cold and calculating. "I'll think about it," he said.

His nonchalant reply angered me. I'd fucking apologized, laid myself bare. I was willing to do anything. Using my vampire speed, I zoomed across the clearing and got into his face. "Now it's your pride and selfishness that's showing!" I screamed in his face, and the voices cut off.

He huffed through his nose, trying to control his wolf, but his eyes went yellow anyway.

"Don't make me draw a line in the sand," I whispered.

I would, I would ask for volunteers, those with me to go to Wolf City, and I would go against him even though he was clearly in charge. He opened his mouth to speak when a small delicate hand brushed his shoulder.

We both turned, blinking out of our rage-fest to see Astra looking up at Rab with an angelic smile. Her mousy brown hair was tucked behind her ears, and she wore a patient and understanding look that neither of us deserved.

"God wants this. She's blessed. She will bring a thousand years of prosperity to our people. I've seen it." She raised her wrist and held the scarred bite mark in his face.

'Pack.' My wolf echoed her gesture and I had to blink back tears at the risk she was taking for me. Making up some prophecy or whatever she was doing to get him to agree.

The trees shook, people whooped, drums even started to beat deeper off into the trees, and Rab gave a resigned nod to Astra. Reaching out, he brushed his thumb across her forehead in a delicate, loving gesture. "Our priestess has spoken!" he bellowed, spinning in a circle.

Priestess? I looked at Astra more closely. Was he talking about her? She was in her midteens, meek, shy, wearing no headdress or fancy regalia.

She simply gave me a small smile.

"Because I trust the mouthpiece of God, I will allow this *city alpha* to prove herself to us." His voice projected into the trees, which shook like a troop of monkeys were rattling their branches.

"And the help? For...the city wolves?" I asked.

He sneered at me. "What does God say of that?" he asked Astra.

She looked at her feet, quiet.

'Please. We need help or thousands will die,' I begged her.

'God does not condone war,' she said to me.

She flicked her gaze up to Rab. "He is quiet on the matter," she told him.

Rab chuckled, shaking his braid. "Then we will be quiet too."

"I'll go!" Arrow stepped into the open circle, grasping

his spear and looking out at the shapes into the trees. "I will go at first light to lend help to the new Wolf City alpha. A new alpha who is different from past ones. When he learned of our crisis, he used his military to give thousands of pounds of food and firewood. I will help that alpha as *he* helped us." He stamped his staff on the ground, and a single tear leaked from my eye.

Arrow knew it wasn't Sawyer who approved that food delivery. It was his dad, but there was too much bad blood there. I could see it. He was trying to make them think differently about this new alpha and I loved him for it. Sawyer was different, and he would be a different alpha than the ones before him.

"I will stand with Arrow." A man came out into the open, wielding a badass-looking blade. All of these men were seriously sculpted from stone, hardened warriors in the best shape of their lives.

"New alpha? What's new about someone who's been bred to hate us for a millennium?" someone yelled from the trees.

Dammit, I wish it were lighter out and I could look that bastard in the eyes.

Thrusting my left hand into the air, I let the light catch on my giant engagement ring. "The new alpha, Sawyer, is my fiancé, my *true mate*." I stopped talking because they'd gasped at that. "And he knows I'm half Paladin. He doesn't care. If we work together, both of our packs can benefit."

It was like it was the knowledge they needed to throw themselves behind the cause. One by one, I heard them.

"I'll go!"

"I'll fight with Arrow."

"Screw the vampires!"

Relief crashed into me. I'd made a promise to Sawyer, and I was keeping it.

Or was I?

I'd said that *I* would be back by morning with warriors. But now...

"Come on, I'll show you to the guesthouse." Astra pulled my hand and it sank into me that I was going to stay here.

Nerves churned in my gut and I'd completely forgotten Sage was there until she stepped over to me, wide-eyed and wearing a half-shredded T-shirt and sweatpants. "You're staying here? What have you done?"

I...followed my heart and it split me in two. Again.

Arrow raised his fist into the air. "Go home and tell the warrior of your household...we leave at dawn!" And a chorus of the Paladin equivalent of an *oorah* rang out, but it was more of a guttural *ouh ouh!*

I walked over to Arrow and stood before him as my wolf nuzzled against his leg. He grinned and dropped his hand down to rub the top of her head. I swear sometimes she was more dog than wolf.

'*I resent that,*' she said, and I bristled, still not used to our bond.

'*Sorry.*'

"Thank you. Truly," I told Arrow.

He bowed his head to me. "Thank *you*. For coming home."

Home. That word on his lips felt so right, so much so that it made a stone sink in my gut. In what world could Sawyer and I get married and live together if I were alpha of these lands? I shook off that problem for future Demi.

I didn't want to ask how many warriors they would get by morning; I just had to trust it would be enough. Arrow, being Rab's brother, seemed to have a lot of pull in the community, and I knew he'd just stuck his neck out for me and I really appreciated it.

I made my hand into a fist and held it out to him. He frowned and I grinned, grabbing his hand and banging them together. "Fist bump. Good night. I'll be up first thing to see you all off."

He chuckled, shaking his head. "City girl."

I smiled and Sage inserted herself between us. "She's marrying my cousin FYI, but *I'm* single."

I smacked her arm and Arrow looked down at her, confused for a second; then her words seemed to dawn on him. "Oh, I'm mated," he said, and Sage frowned, stepping away from him with a pout. Every male here was distracting eye candy. I wasn't going to deny that, and clearly Sage had noticed.

"You are? I'd love to meet her," I told him as movement picked up behind us and everyone started to disperse. I'd always felt a brotherly vibe from Arrow. Was he hot? Yes. But he was sweet and helpful and... totally in the friend zone.

"Tomorrow morning, at first light," he told me, and then Astra was back, tugging my hand.

"Alpha, come. I've been working on your guest home for weeks. Come and see." She pulled me away and Sage and I followed her.

Weeks?

I shared a look with Sage.

"I knew you would come." Astra grinned as she pulled me into the dark trees past where the floodlights had brightened the meadow, and we were plunged into darkness again, only the moon to light our path. There was a flagstone walkway covered in moss, and suddenly my eyes adjusted, noticing the appearance of hundreds of people to the left and right of the path. Some were climbing down from the trees where they had perched; others just stood, arms crossed, talking in hushed tones and watching me closely.

Every three feet was a little solar garden light that lit our path—and also the faces of some seriously pissed-off women.

"Taking our men off to war already, *Alpha*?" one snapped as I passed by.

I ignored her and yanked on Sage's arm when she opened her mouth to retort. It wasn't the time. I needed to go into a dark room and tell Sawyer what was going on and then cry myself to sleep. My wolf leaped into my chest then, and I nodded for Astra to lead the way. I was ready to see where Run had grown up, the land I was supposed to heal and the place in which I was going to lead these people, should I be found worthy.

———•·•———

The path led for a good twenty minutes before the dim lights of a bustling village shone in the distance. Sage and I shared a look.

Whoa.

I didn't know why I expected grass huts and torches. The wall encompassing the Paladin land was made of a deep red brick and stood strong, over seven feet tall. Two ornately decorated wrought iron gates stood open, with two soft lights on top of the pillars that held each gate. Again, each light had a tiny solar panel at the top, like the ones you would get for your garden at Home Depot. It wasn't a strong light, just enough to illuminate the buildings' shapes and walkways, but I was impressed. Astra skipped along the path to the gates and nodded at the two guards that stood there.

"Told you she'd come!" Astra told them.

Their eyes ran over Sage and me both. "These two city wolves have your permission to be here, Priestess?" one of them asked with a sneer. His pec twitched and Sage and I shared a look.

Man, these guys were ripped. They must work out all day long and eat zero carbs, because there wasn't an ounce of fat on them.

Astra rolled her eyes. "It's our *alpha*! She came!"

My heart broke at her words, and I could see Sage's eyes getting misty. The way she spoke about me, her tone—it was full of reverence and excitement and *absolute* trust.

The guards stepped aside, glaring at me with suspicion.

Priestess. That word again. I'd had no idea when we'd met Astra in the cages of the dark fey realm that we'd met the priestess of the Paladin people. Everyone seemed to defer to her, even over Rab. Which was surprising since she was so young and meek.

The second we were in the gates, Astra turned right, heading down a small lane, and we passed house after house, all relatively the same size and the same deep red brick with a thick brown muddy concrete between the lines. The bricks looked hand packed, not machine-made, as each one wasn't exactly perfect, but the masonry was beautiful. The homes stood sturdily with handblown glass windows and clay shingle roofs. I felt like I was in Europe or something. This quaint village had such exquisite artistry that if it were photographed, it would earn the appreciation of many people in the human world. Each home had little flower boxes outside what I assumed was the kitchen window. They hung full of herbs I recognized—rosemary, chives, cilantro.

Although I was enchanted with this village, with each step I was dreading having to tell Sawyer what I'd just done, so I stalled by asking Astra about the buildings.

"Did you guys build these or...?" I let my question linger.

Astra nodded. "We make everything here—bricks, cement, glass, ironwork. Our loom broke, which is why we needed the blankets," she explained.

I bobbed my head as I took in everything around me. It was...clean, rustic, beautiful. Natural ground cover dotted the side of the walking path with rich ferns and tall grasses, and each home was landscaped lightly with whatever trees and plants were there when they moved in. It looked like they hadn't moved a single blade of grass or fern, and built their homes into the landscape. But as I looked closer in the moonlight, I noticed some of the leaves looked burned, curled in with a black fuzz encasing them.

I stopped, leaning forward to inspect it.

"Plant death. Started when Red Moon died. The alpha's power bleeds from the land and this will cover the crops until we have nothing left. Our people will sicken next." Astra's voice came from behind me and my heart squeezed.

Plant death.

After Red died.

This was…my fault. For weeks I'd been in Wolf City just gallivanting around in my Range Rover with my giant engagement ring, and they were…

My hand went to my throat as I whimpered.

"The village is beautiful. Do you have running water?" Sage asked quickly, noticing my discomfort and changing the subject, for which I was grateful.

Astra nodded. "Of course." She pointed off in the distance. "The men fill the gravity-fed water tower once a month from the lake, and we have an electric pump fed by solar. We are completely off-grid here, as you might call it in the city." I followed her line of sight and thought I saw the outline of something, but it was too hard to tell in this light.

Guilt gnawed at my gut, and I could tell from Sage's pained face that it got her thinking as well.

City life in essence was…frivolous and definitely not off-grid.

"Here we are!" Astra bounced up and down in front of an adorable little redbrick cottage with a bright blue door. "I've been filling the pantry all day with the freeze-dried food you gave us and got some blankets in there too. I knew you would come home." She threw herself forward and wrapped her arms around me again, squeezing me tightly, and I couldn't hold back the tears anymore. Maybe it was our connection, maybe I was just tired, or turning into a total wuss, but Astra had the most innocent soul and I couldn't take it anymore.

When she pulled back, I wiped my eyes quickly and had to swallow my sob.

"Astra...thank you. This is very kind. Where do you sleep?"

She pointed to a building directly across from my guesthouse. "In there, obviously."

My gaze ran the length of the giant building. It was the size of ten of the little cottages. The large, rectangular structure was covered with dark red brick; the clay tiled roof shot high up into the sky. There was no cross or anything like that on top, but it looked like a church.

It had the pointed top like the ones I saw in Spokane, near Delphi.

Sage and I shared a look but said nothing. Did Astra...hold church services here? Were the Paladins a religious people? They sure talked about God a lot. Was a priestess in the Paladin culture like a pastor? I was so fascinated.

"Well, I'm exhausted." Sage yawned and I concurred, pulling myself from my thoughts. We bid Astra good night and stepped inside the small guest home.

It was adorable and simple and absolutely perfect. Everything was handcrafted with expert care. The couch was a wrought iron bench with huge plush padding that had been dyed a bright yellow. The coffee table was wrought iron as well, with blown glass. It had little bubbles and swirls, which gave it a rich artistry.

"So you're staying?" Sage turned and looked at me.

She emptied her face of emotion, but I could hear the disappointment in her voice.

I just didn't have the energy for this right now. Especially knowing I had to also have this fight with Sawyer.

I sighed. "Let's talk in the morning. I'm beat."

She nodded, yawning again. "Fine. All of the guys are insanely hot here. I know what I'll be dreaming about tonight."

I chuckled. "What about Walsh?"

"Who?" she joked, before disappearing into a room with a wink. I heard the *oof* of breath leave her as she seemingly leaped into a bed, then I went in search of another room. Down the hall, past a bathroom, I found a light blue blanket draped over a wrought iron four-poster bed. I collapsed onto the thick cotton mattress, kicking off my shoes.

Rolling onto my back, I stared up at the plaster ceiling. It had been dyed a light yellow and I wondered where they got the dye from. Turmeric? Or did they barter for paint? It was incredible to see a self-sufficient place like this...

I was stalling by thinking of other things rather than mind texting Sawyer.

I had to get this over with. Taking a deep breath, I sent him a message. *'The Paladins will help.'*

Relief coursed through our bond from him and seeped into me.

'*Oh, thank fuck, Demi. Now get back here before I lose my mind.*' I felt his anxiety and also grief, probably over his father.

Silent tears rolled down my cheeks and onto the pillow. '*Sawyer...I...told them I would stay and help in exchange for—*'

'*Don't fuck with me like that. I'm too fragile right now,*' he interrupted, and I winced.

This was going to be harder than I thought.

'*I'm serious. They won't help us unless I step up to the plate and claim my alpha heritage.*'

'*Demi, I will cut off my own foot, remove this ankle bracelet, hobble into the woods, and drag you back here if you tell me you are serious again.*'

I gulped. '*I'm...serious.*' I thought of the plant death. '*Sawyer, their land is dying. They aren't like the city wolves. Their power is—*'

'*Woman, you're going to kill me.*' He cut me off with an exasperated sigh that bled throughout our bond, bringing with it feelings of helplessness. '*I'm going to go fully gray and die of heartbreak.*'

'*Sawyer, listen. Their power is tied to the alpha. And their land. They need me to survive,*' I pressed, and he was quiet for a whole minute.

'*Demi, I'm in the middle of a war right now. I can't really have an entire conversation. Will I see you in the morning or no?*'

My throat pinched with unshed emotion.

'No. But obviously—'

'No?' I felt his pain slice into my chest. 'Demi, your parents are hiding in a bomb shelter. Raven just got here asking about you. I'm waiting for my future wife to show up so I can wrap my arms around her as I bury my father in the ground, and now you tell me you're not coming back? What am I supposed to do with that?'

For someone who couldn't have a conversation right now, he sure was chatty. Guilt wormed its way into my gut. He was right, it was awful—I was fucking awful for doing this to him in the middle of a war with his father dead. But... 'Sawyer, they wouldn't help without me giving them something. Their land is dying, the people are hurting, and I'm not just going to leave them. It's not who I am, and not who you fell in love with.'

I felt him soften. Tender feelings of love and compassion bled into me.

'Okay, babe, I get it, but I can't just traipse into the woods and camp out with you there. I'm alpha, my father just died, we are at war, and I have an ankle monitor on that we still can't get off. What do you expect me to do?'

My heart panged at the mention of his father again. I wanted to be there with him, and I still didn't know what this alpha stuff required of me. 'I know, and this won't be like last time when I got lost in the Magic Lands. I can come see you. I'll send the warriors in the morning at first light, and then I'll check things out here and see *how I can help. By tomorrow night I can zip back over and see you again and we can come up with a plan.'*

There was silence and I felt his attention divided. Finally he spoke back to me, his voice strained.

'Zip back over? Demi, my love, we are at war. Our woods are on fire. They've just released dark fey into the school grounds and the Ithaki are getting involved. It's now or never. Come home and you can go to the Paladins after the war settles down, after my ankle bracelet comes off. I'll go with you. I'll live in a tent by your side, do whatever it takes, my love—just not now.'

A sob ripped from my chest, and I had to slap a hand over my mouth to muffle it.

'Sawyer, the land is blackened and dying. They aren't like your wolves. They will start to get sick too if I don't step up to my responsibilities. I have to be here right now.'

He was silent so damn long I had to call his name again.

'Sawyer?'

I felt my agony mix with his, merging together through our bond, coalescing like a tornado, threatening to rip us both in two.

'Demi, loving you means I support whatever your desires are. If you really want to stay there and...help the Paladin people, then...I support you.'

My heart felt heavy, like a stone in my chest. Sawyer was the epitome of the perfect man and I felt like I was letting him down.

'*We will be together soon. I promise,*' I assured him.

'*I gotta go now. Read the note I gave you, okay?*' He sounded disappointed, but there was nothing more I could say. I'd completely forgotten about the note he'd shoved in my pocket when I'd seen him in the war room in his parents' house.

'*I will. I love you, Sawyer. I love you so much. Thanks for supporting me.*'

'*Good night, Demi. I love you too.*'

I lay there for a moment letting this hollow feeling spread from my chest through my limbs. There was no good way out of this situation. It sucked no matter what. Either way, someone was going to be disappointed.

Reaching into my pocket, I pulled out the letter and sat up, leaning into the window and letting the outside porch light cast its glow onto the white paper.

I unfolded it, confused about what it was and how he could have written me a letter before he even knew I was coming here. He'd have had no time between the vampire attack at the hotel and getting his mother back to his house after his father's death.

The second I saw his cursive script across the page, I finally let the sobs free.

Engagement speech was scrolled across the top.

He'd written a speech for our special night, something I hadn't even thought to do—one he never got to read.

My heart pounded against my chest as I read the next line.

Demi, loving you is easy.

From the first day I met you, I saw your strength, your fire, and a little bit of your pain.

Tears streamed down my face and onto the paper.

And I knew that day that I had met my equal, my better half.

Where I am hard and unyielding, you are soft and forgiving. Where my mind thinks in straight lines and squares, yours thinks in swirls and arcs.

Demi, we are not exact copies of each other, but we are perfect for one another. You are the one I choose to love, the one I choose to place all my bets on, my future wife.

You love your family and friends with a loyal fierceness that gives me pride to watch, and I am lucky enough to be one of those people.

Thank you for choosing me. Thank you for saying yes.

I burst into tears then, my vision blurry as I read the last line.

(Now kiss her.)

I fell back onto the pillow, clutching the letter in my hands, and sobbed into the blanket as my emotions overwhelmed me. I just wanted to marry him and be normal.

But there was no *normal* here, no going back now. We were at war, and if I was honest, my time running for my life through the Magic Lands had changed me. I was a fighter, a survivor, a Paladin alpha. I couldn't just ignore that and sit back in a glass castle with Sawyer and be his wife.

I *did* want to be his wife, I wanted a life with him, but I had my own path to walk too, and the agony of not knowing an immediate solution for Sawyer and my relationship tore at me until I finally dozed off.

CHAPTER TWO

S AGE WOKE ME WHILE IT WAS STILL DARK OUT. I'D
had to pull myself from the comfortable bed and
brush my teeth quickly before rushing outside. Murmured
low voices came from the church across the street. Sage
and I crossed the brick walkway and I balked at the
sight of nearly a thousand warriors. They were all bare
chested despite the chilly air breezing through the town,
and they held a variety of deadly looking weapons. The
bright blue streaks of paint across their faces and chests
gave me chills. These men were true warriors. You could
see it in their eyes, the way they not only looked like
they weren't afraid of death, but they welcomed it. Most
of the warriors were men, but I spied a few women, just
as deadly and fierce looking.

Arrow and Rab were talking animatedly to each
other, while Astra had her hands on a man's shoulders as

she seemingly prayed for him. Being in such a different culture was fascinating. I wanted to know everything about the Paladins and their customs, but now was not the time to learn. Footsteps sounded behind me, and I turned to see a large pack of wolves coming down the street, a hundred of them or more.

These wolves were large, larger than our city wolves, and all black, with bits of rust fur at the tips.

"Paladin wolves," Sage whispered.

Oh.

"What if someone attacks us while you're gone? You're taking our best warriors!" Rab shouted, and I turned my attention back to the front of the church.

"They want to show the new alpha that they will fight for her cause," Arrow stated passionately. "They have faith that she will heal our lands and people and not leave us."

Guilt shot through me. These people that I didn't even know were willing to fight for me so that I would help them. It just reaffirmed that I couldn't go back to Sawyer until I had given my all here and helped them.

"I don't trust her. She'll leave when it gets hard," Rab growled. As if sensing me, he glared behind him and met my cold gaze.

I shouldn't have stayed and eavesdropped, but dammit that comment made me mad, and they were talking loud enough for the whole damn group to hear.

"The hell I will!" I shouted, and bounded over to

29

them in long angry strides, earning the gaze of over a hundred warriors who stood the closest. "You don't know *anything* about me. You have no idea what I'm capable of." I felt my wolf come to the surface then, and Rab spun fully, looking me straight in the eyes.

"Well, *little wolf*," he sneered. "Half of our warriors are leaving, and if we get attacked by the Ithaki while they are gone, I will *personally* hold you responsible for every death."

Moving warriors from one place to another and leaving the Paladins vulnerable was not ideal, but I had to choose the lesser of two evils. Right now, the city wolves were stuck in a bomb shelter. Clearly that situation was more dire.

"I wouldn't expect anything less. Now, how can I help here?"

"Demi," Sage called from behind me, voice thick with concern. "Aren't you going to even help me lead the warriors back to Wolf City?"

Fuck. I should have told her this morning.

I turned and faced her, tears welling in my eyes. "I...I need to stay here for the time being," I told my redheaded bestie.

Her eyes widened as she looked behind me at the warriors. "Demi, Wolf City...Sawyer. We *need* you right now."

Being torn like this, it was awful. I gestured to the blackened grass at my feet, and the dying cornfields off in the distance, which I could see even from here were tipped with black char. "No. You want me. But *they* need me." I lowered my voice. "I'm going to stay for a few days and talk about next steps with them. I want to earn their trust, do what I can to heal them," I told her sincerely. She didn't get it; she didn't understand these were my people too.

She frowned. "Fine. I'll stay with you." She crossed her arms in defiance.

Tears pricked at my eyes as I shook my head. "I need you to lead the warriors to Sawyer. I told him you're coming." I tapped my head.

It was early as all hell, we were both exhausted, but war didn't wait for you to get a good night's sleep.

"Fine. I'll drop them off and come right back," she growled.

"Sage—"

"Stop arguing with me, you stubborn ass. I'm not leaving you here with hottie alphahole over there." She narrowed her eyes at Rab and I grinned.

Any and all hotness Rab possessed was eaten away by his asshole personality. Besides, I was only interested in Sawyer.

That didn't mean I couldn't admire the chiseled bodies every now and then though.

"Alright. See you tonight, then?" I asked.

Her frown grew deeper. "You told Sawyer you're staying and that I'm going?"

31

My heart pinched. "It was the worst thing I'd ever had to tell him...but yes. Last night."

She nodded. "I'll be back tonight, then, maybe tomorrow."

We hugged and my throat tightened with emotion. Why did I feel like I wouldn't see her for a long time? War was ugly, and everything felt so dire on both sides of the border. I hoped I was making the right choice by staying behind with the Paladins. The thing was, the city wolves had Sawyer and these people had no one.

"Be safe," I told her.

She wiped at her eyes and then walked over to Arrow. "Come on, I'll show you the way."

A female warrior stepped up to Arrow, her body nearly as chiseled as his, her breasts covered by a tiny triangle strip of suede that hung from a string that was covered in pretty red beads. She had a deadly grip on her weapon, and I knew instantly that this was Arrow's mate. He seemed like the type who would go for a warrior woman.

The men started to disperse, and I thought I should say something, give them confidence in my abilities, although I had no idea what would be required of me.

"I *won't* let you down," I said in a strong voice that surprisingly didn't shake.

The men looked from Astra, back to me, and then nodded, heading off to fight a war they'd never started or believed in.

I stood there, watching every single man and wolf pass by me, and gave them a tight smile. When the last warrior finally turned around the corner, Rab stepped over to me, arms crossed as he pinned me with a glare.

"Three thousand, one hundred, and seventy-eight."

I swallowed hard. "What?"

"That's how many warriors just left. That's how many Paladins you have decided to put at risk on your first day as trial alpha." His eyes flashed yellow.

"Trial alpha?" I crossed my arms and glowered at him. Clearly, Arrow was the nice brother. "Last time I checked, I'm the *only* alpha you got."

He chuckled, looking over at Astra. "You haven't told her anything, have you?"

Astra squirmed, adjusting her cream linen top with nervous fingers. "I told her what was important at the time."

My stomach dropped, and my face must have shown it too, because Rab grinned. "You have no idea what you're in for, *city girl*."

He blasted past me, nearly knocking into me, and I was left staring at Astra with what I hoped she interpreted as a stunned expression.

"Come on. Let's go in and talk." She nodded to the large double doors of the giant redbrick church.

I squirmed. Not exactly what I wanted to do right now. But I needed some answers. Following her up the steps, I looked back over my shoulder as the sun began to rise, casting buttery orange light over the Paladin village. It was so…stunning…and yet…clearly dying. Hundreds of the small redbrick cottages dotted the landscape, all built in straight little rows. In the distance were the open fields. Black sludgy stuff marred the tips of the corn and other crops. The trees looked…ashy…like they had been burned. The plant death covered everything. As Astra led me inside, I did a quick check-in with Sawyer.

'Sage and over three thousand warriors are on their way to you now. I'm going to do my best to help out here today and see if I can get back over to you tomorrow for a visit.'

His reply was immediate. *'No. It's too dangerous, just stay there. I'm sending Eugene to protect you. He should reach you in a couple hours.'*

I wanted to argue that I didn't need protecting here, but I knew it would make him feel better to send someone to look after me. It made me sick that neither of us knew when we would see each other again. *'Alright. Everything okay there?'*

It was a stupid thing to ask. What could be okay about a war?

'My mom, your parents, and Raven's family are safe. So that's good.'

That sounded an awful lot like good news–bad news talk.

'And the bad news?'

I could hear him internally sigh, and desperation bled

through our imprint. *'It's bad, Demi. I'm glad you're not here to see the fall of everything my father helped build.'*

Oh God. I sagged in the doorway as Astra waited patiently for me to join her inside.

'Sawyer. Tell me. I can come back. I can help.'

'No. Stay there. The three thousand men will be a big help. I gotta go.'

He pulled away from me and I was left with my mind spinning. What the hell was I supposed to do now? My fiancé was in crisis and I was helpless to do anything.

"Everything okay, Alpha?" Astra wrung her hands nervously and I felt her trepidation through our bond.

I sighed. The entirety of Magic City was at war and I was pretty sure that war started because of me, and my fiancé was left dealing with it all, but bitching about it wasn't going to help anyone. "Let's just talk about how I can help here."

Astra nodded, her brown hair bobbing. "Come on in."

She stepped deeper into the space and behind a row of pews. I stepped inside and allowed myself to examine the space further.

Rows and rows of thickly lacquered, dark wood pews lined the giant room from the front to the back. Astra wove in and out of the aisles, making her way to a stage up at the front. It had church vibes in the way it was laid out, but I could see no religious insignia or idols.

35

We arrived at the stage and I peered at the glowing light coming from it. I expected to see a cross or something of that nature, but instead there were hundreds of flickering candles.

"One protection prayer for each soldier who left," she informed me.

My eyes widened.

Over three thousand tea lights? That must have taken all night.

She walked across the hardwood floors and toward the flickering stage as I let my eyes go to the windows at the top of the building. There was more of that homemade-looking glass. It was no Roman Catholic cathedral but there was a good vibe to the place, peaceful.

Astra stepped up onto the stage and I followed her. Now that we were close to the candles, I could feel their collective heat, admiring the lights as they flickered and swayed. They were stacked on little risers in ascending order.

Astra reached into a little box on the side of the stage and set one more tea light down on a space she found on the floor. Then she clasped her hands and muttered under her breath. I stood there watching her, thinking about when she'd healed Walsh and how that magical blue glitter stuff had fallen from the sky and onto her body. She'd literally saved his life with her power. I also thought about how they'd called her priestess. That was a word the witches used, but she was clearly a wolf...a spiritual or religious one.

She baffled me, but in a good way.

Looking up from her clasped hands, she waved her fingers over the small candle and a flame burst from the wick. I sucked in a breath at the display of magic.

"That was for Sage," she told me, acting like she didn't just do something super cool and amazing like light a freaking candle with her mind!

"Are you...part witch?" I was trying to figure this all out. Figure *her* out.

She scowled. "The witches are evil. They've turned away from the Father and use their magic to power the darkness."

Okay... I didn't know what that meant. "The Father...being...?"

She frowned. "The Father of all creation. God. Prime Creator."

I nodded. "Right. That's what I thought."

"Can all Paladins light candles with a wave of their hands?" I looked at my own fingers, wondering if it were possible. She barked out a laugh and it made her look much younger. Now I questioned my guesstimate of her age.

"Obviously not!" She laughed some more, the lightness causing my own lips to curl.

I shifted on the balls of my feet nervously as the candles flickered shadows across her face. "I don't really know anything about Paladins, Astra. I was raised among humans."

She frowned, grasping at her chest as if I'd just told her my grandmother died. "Shells of their former selves. May that never happen to us. You have to help us," she pleaded.

What the what?

I frowned, opening my arms. "I'm here. I have no idea what you need from me, but I'm here. Just help me understand everything."

She nodded. "This way. I'll explain everything."

Why did that give me a sinking feeling in my stomach?

CHAPTER THREE

I FOLLOWED HER PAST THE CANDLES TO THE BACK OF the stage where there was a door. She opened it and descended a row of creaky stairs. Stepping after her and down into the basement, I passed flame sconces that lit up the walls and I wondered if it was normal fire or that magic fire she'd made with her hands. Could she snap her fingers and make them blow out?

Probably...

When we reached the bottom steps, I took in the large space. To the right was a bedroom with the door ajar and a simple four-poster bed. On the back wall was a fireplace with crackling logs inside. There was a little kitchen off to the left and a sitting area in front of the fire. In the farthest corner of the room was a small floor pillow facing a low table or altar. One single thick blue candle burned on the altar with a vibrant purple flame.

She pointed to the purple flickering glow. "That's a blessing candle. For you. I've prayed for you every night since you saved me from the dark fey and brought me home."

I swallowed hard, feeling slightly uncomfortable at her kind gesture. Why? I had no idea. This girl had so much faith in me. I didn't want to let her down.

I was about to respond when she spoke again.

"When Running Spirit was killed…" She shook her head. "No, I need to go back further. Let me start over." She rubbed her hands together nervously. "My mother, Faye, was a priestess too. Blessed with healing like me."

She gestured for me to sit down on the couch and I did, facing her as she snuggled in across from me. Being with Astra felt so…easy. Which was weird considering I literally knew nothing about her.

'*Pack*,' my wolf told me, and I nodded. Astra was pack; that's why we felt like sisters. It was similar to my imprint with Sawyer, the closeness, the reading of her energy but in a familial way. She was nervous now but also excited.

"Was?" I asked, wondering if her mother was…

"Dead." She nodded, and then pointed to the ceiling. "With the Father now."

Right…

"I'm sorry."

She swallowed hard. "She died shortly after Red Moon, your grandfather, passed."

40

I frowned. "That was recent. How did she die, if you don't mind my asking?"

She looked around the home as if still expecting to see her mother walk out of the kitchen. When she met my gaze, I wasn't prepared for the fear I saw in her eyes.

"Don't run off or anything, okay? Just hear me out first." She inched closer to me as if she were preparing to jump out and grab me when I inevitably tried to bolt.

My heart picked up speed then, thumping wildly against my chest. "Why would I run?" I swallowed hard.

"My mom died shortly after Red Moon because...we as priestesses cannot live long without being tethered to an alpha." She raised her wrist to show the marks I'd made there when I'd claimed her and now it all made sense.

My heart rate slowed a little. I'd been expecting so much worse. Like, I don't know...for her to tell me she needed my kidney or something for a spell.

"Okay, well, are we tethered now? I mean, you're okay, right?" It dawned on me that she might be about to drop a bomb and tell me that she was about to die.

She nodded. "I'm good now that you've claimed me and we are tethered."

Whew. "Cool."

She chewed her lip. "But the rest of the pack will lose their magic if you don't claim them as well. Their wolves will slowly die until they become weak humans. Our land has already started dying."

I squirmed. This was nothing she hadn't basically

told me before, and I'd accepted when I said I would stay and help that I'd have to become alpha of these people. Claiming them all? It was a bit much, but if it would save their magic...

"I'll do it," I said, waiting for the relief to show on her face.

The look never came. Instead her mouth twisted into a grimace.

"What's wrong?"

She reached out and grasped my hands. "In order to become our alpha, you have to prove yourself to the land, the magic, the people, the Father."

I could actually feel the frown pulling my face into a scowl. Is that why Rab called me a trial alpha? He didn't think I could pass the test or whatever?

Oh, fuck that. The best way to make sure I did something was to tell me I wasn't capable.

"Bring it," I told her. "I'll prove myself."

She squeezed my hands, giving me a small smile. "You are so brave, Alpha. I knew the second I met you that you and your lineage would be the one to lead us for generations. I believe in you."

Nervousness crawled through me and I wondered if it was me or her. "So what do I need to do to prove this? A fight?"

I didn't want to kill Rab. He was Arrow's brother, and although he was a bit of a douchebag, I knew he was just protecting his people.

She sighed. "You will have to journey through the Dark Woods alone, to the Cave of Magic."

I gulped. Alone? Dark Woods? Cave of Magic? Okay, shit just got a little scarier than I was expecting. "What's in the cave?"

Astra shrugged. "I don't know. The only people to make it back alive are dead now."

My eyes widened. "Red Moon?"

She nodded. "And Run, your father. Only alphas can enter the Dark Woods and go searching for the cave."

"Biological father," I corrected her, not wanting to discount the man who raised me, the man I considered to be my dad.

She bobbed her head up and down. "It's supposed to be a three-day journey in and out...if you don't get lost." She paused and I raised an eyebrow.

"Get lost? Has anyone ever...gotten lost?" Her hands clamped down on mine as if willing me to stay on this couch with her. Then her eyes seared into my soul with an astonishing flaming gold as her wolf came to the surface.

"Run got lost...and came back three years later. Some say the Dark Woods will hide the cave from you, only revealing it when you are ready. You could be gone years."

What. The. Fuck. Did she just say?

I yanked my hands out of hers and stood, backing up to the wall. "Whoa, you never said anything about being gone *years*."

She shook her head. "It's just a possibility."

Hah! I barked out a laugh. "I could just *possibly* get lost for three years? No way." I pointed to the ring on my finger. "I am marrying the love of my life, and if I am gone for three years, his entire family will die, *including him*, because of a curse *your* people put on him!" I yelled and she bowed her head in submission, which made me immediately feel guilty.

"Shit, I'm sorry." I stepped closer to her, then rubbed my face, trying not to have a panic attack. Dark Woods for three years to save thousands of people? Pass. HARD PASS. "I just...I can't, Astra. It's asking too much. If you could guarantee me I would be in and out in three days, I would totally do it, but the thought of getting lost for years... I can't."

A single tear slipped from her eye, and she wiped it away with the back of her hand. Turning back to face me, she walked over to the little wooden altar she had set up and kneeled before the purple flickering candle, clasping her hands and muttering unintelligible words under her breath.

I sat there awkwardly, unsure what to do when she stood, a smile back on her face. "I understand, Demi, and I respect your choice. Let me give you a tour? See if you can help in another way?"

I frowned.

She called me *Demi*, not Alpha, and it felt like a slap in the face, but I ignored it.

"Absolutely. I can totally help in other ways. Food, goods, I mean whatever you need, I can get them when the war dies down."

She nodded and we stepped out of the room and back up the stairs.

———·•·———

Two hours later, I knew exactly what she'd done. She didn't give me a tour, she threw my heart into a blender and hit pulse. I'd been through the dying wheat fields, the rotten corn crops, the completely foul fruit orchard, all black with disease, all screaming: *You are a piece of shit if you don't go into the Dark Woods and heal this land.*

"The land is dying from the loss of the alpha's magic, which is tied to it. That can only happen when the trial alpha reaches the Cave of Magic," Astra had told me as we'd walked through the putrid cornfield.

I'd just nodded at first, ignoring her apparent sales pitch. But then she brought me to the birthing center. There were over two hundred women currently pregnant, and when Astra set one of the brand-new babies in my arms, I frowned when I noticed something was off with the child. He seemed happy enough but...I couldn't put my finger on it.

I stared down at him, so small and innocent, while I tried to figure out what was nagging at my brain.

Weeping came from the room down the hall as Astra leaned in close to me. "Born without a wolf. It will happen until our new alpha goes through the rite of passage, finds the cave, and shows they are worthy and claims the land and people."

I stared at her in horror, and then back at the baby. The eyes. *It was the eyes!* They were…brown. Beautiful brown baby eyes, but…not the magical blue of the Paladin people. I inhaled, smelling the baby.

Human.

"Are you telling me that two Paladins just gave birth to a human?" I whisper-screamed to her. How the hell was that possible? Even a Paladin and a human would have a child that could shift into wolf form.

Astra nodded, stroking the boy's forehead lovingly as I held him. "Not enough magic to go around now that Red is gone."

The guilt of her words hit me like a ton of bricks. I quickly handed her the baby before the sob ripped from my throat. Then I ran down the hall and burst out of the door. The cool breeze hit my face as I thought of what that poor mother must be going through. What that child would live with. Was being human awful? No, but to grow up different, among wolves and not being able to shift or heal, he'd be a freak. Because of me. He was a beautiful, healthy baby boy, but he wasn't a wolf, not like he should be. My breath came in and out in ragged gasps as I surveyed the dying land before me. What I'd seen today were good people, a hardworking people who didn't deserve to lose their magic, their wolves, all because I was scared of being gone too long.

'I need to see you. I have to talk to you about something in person. It's important,' I told Sawyer as the panic threatened to fully take hold of me.

His reply was immediate. *'Are you okay?'*

Tears streamed down my face. I couldn't imagine losing my wolf, not now that I knew she was the one reason I was left living, that she was my protector when Vicon and his buddies took my virginity against my will.

'No. I'm not. I need to see you, Sawyer.'

'Alright, I'll have Eugene escort you back to me when he gets there, but can you bring some protection? Maybe twenty Paladins? The Wild Lands are crawling with Ithaki and vampires right now.'

Ask more people to risk their lives for me? Sure thing.

'Okay,' I said.

'Okay...see you tonight.'

"You okay?" a familiar voice called behind me, and I quickly wiped my tears and spun on my heel.

Rab. I sighed when I saw him. "Come to gloat at my emotional weakness?"

He shrugged. "I came to see if you were hungry. My mate just made lunch. She wants to meet you."

I internally groaned, looking to the door of the birthing center, where Astra waved me off.

"I'll meet up with you later!" she said, as if she'd overheard us.

"Sure," I told him, wondering why he would invite me to lunch after he was such a dick to me before. Why would his mate want to meet me? Hopefully, she was nothing like him. I wasn't in the mood to dine with *two* assholes.

We walked across the burned blades of grass. It looked like a recent fire had scorched the land, but Astra had explained it was just the sudden loss of alpha magic when Red died.

Rab gave me a long side-glance and I growled. "What?"

He chuckled. "I can't believe our last remaining alpha is a city wolf."

I rolled my eyes. "I can't believe you're related to sweet and charming Arrow."

His lips twitched into a half grin and then fell. "I can't believe Red died so that you could live…"

I stopped walking, my throat tightening as his words. "Hey, that was a low blow."

He shook his head. "No, what I meant was…I can't believe that Red crossed over Ithaki land to save a city wolf who happened to be his long-lost granddaughter."

Oh.

"Yes, it was…synchronistic."

He shook his head. "I don't think so," he sighed, looking deeply into my eyes before inhaling through his nose, as if smelling me. "I think he knew. I think on some level he knew who you were."

I had to bite the inside of my cheek to keep from crying. I wished I had gotten to meet the old man, to know him. I tried to think back to our conversation, and any indication that he knew we were related.

"Rab! Food's getting cold. Get your butt in here!" a female yelled down the street, and I grinned at the sassy way she spoke to him.

"Oh, I'm going to like her." I let the amusement play out on my features as he scowled at me. He stalked off toward the beautiful woman standing in the red doorway who was waving us over, and I followed him.

As we approached, I examined her closer. She looked to be about midtwenties with her brown hair in a long silky braid over one shoulder. She had those intense almond-shaped turquoise eyes, and a smattering of freckles across her nose that made her look young and innocent. I swallowed hard when my gaze went to her abdomen and I noticed her belly was swollen with pregnancy.

"Hello, Demi. I'm Willow." She smiled at me and bowed her head slightly in greeting.

"You're pregnant," I said stupidly, instead of actually greeting her like a normal person. That's why she invited me; she didn't want her baby to be born human. This was all a part of their plan.

Oh Lord.

The guilt trip was being laid so thick I could barely breathe.

She nodded. "Only four months along, but yeah." She grinned at Rab. He reached over and rubbed her belly as the smells of something savory filtered out to us on the porch.

"Come on in." She stepped back and ushered me inside.

I gingerly crossed the threshold, the guilt of her unborn baby weighing on me with each step. If I didn't go into the Dark Woods and find that damn cave, then her baby would be born human...without a wolf.

I swallowed hard, looking around her home. It was similar to my guest cottage but seemed more lived-in. She had the table set with some type of bean stew and a fresh bowl of rice. The tablecloth was a deep red, and there were some dried husks of wheat for decoration in the centerpiece. "Sorry there is nothing fresh. As you know, the crops have been failing since we lost Red."

I paled.

"Dry rice and beans, courtesy of *Wolf City*," Rab grumbled.

Willow reached out and smacked him on the back of the head. "What's gotten into you, mate? Where is your gratitude? Would you rather your pregnant mate starve?"

Rab's cheeks pinked and he cleared his throat. "Thank you for the food," he half growled and sat down.

I liked her, but I frowned at Rab as we both sat down

at the table. "You're welcome, *Rab*." I said his name like it was made of poison as Willow served me a plate of steaming hot beans and rice. There was also a spicy looking relish on the side.

Willow barked out a laugh. "You know his name is Rabid Wolf for a reason, right?" She bared her teeth in a mock growl and he playfully smacked her butt.

I chortled, my mouth going slack. "Rab is short for *Rabid*!"

He squared his shoulders, shoving a mouthful of beans into his mouth. "It's a strong name."

Yeah, for an asshole, which he was, but there was a playfulness to our banter and I relaxed into that.

"Demi needs a Paladin name." Willow mixed her rice and beans as I started to take a bite.

"She needs to earn it. It's not given out for free," Rab said through gritted teeth.

Willow rolled her eyes at her mate. "I'm aware of that. Who says she can't earn it?"

I tipped my chin to her in thanks but Rab laughed. "Astra and Arrow both risked their lives to sneak into Wolf City and plead with her to help us and she gave them canned food and turned them away. That's not the trait of an alpha."

"Hey!" I slammed my fist down on the table and the glasses clanked, causing everyone to jump. "I'm sorry." I looked at Willow, but she seemed unbothered by my outburst.

Then I glared at Rab: "I only found out I was *half* Paladin a few months ago, and an alpha a few weeks ago. Excuse me for having to think things through before throwing away my entire life to help people who have been nothing but assholes to me and my mate." I shoved my engagement ring in his face. "The mate that I need to rush and marry so he doesn't die from the curse your people put on his family!"

The table went silent, and I didn't realize how loud I'd gotten, but I'd definitely screamed the last part. Rab sighed, looking down at his food in an apparent act of submission. Willow's gaze flicked over to my ring and she grinned. "I love her. She'll be a perfect alpha."

I yanked my hand back and rubbed my face. "I'm sorry I lost my temper—"

Willow snort-laughed. "You're a Paladin female. We would expect nothing less."

I gave her a small smile, grateful to feel so accepted but still annoyed Rab and everyone expected me to just ride in and save the day the second they told me they needed help.

"The curse on the Hudson family was a mistake," Rab finally said. "A mistake our entire people have lived with for as long as I can remember."

Fair enough. We all made mistakes, but the curse was still there and a huge problem in Sawyer's life. "Well, you can't expect someone to just easily get over that mistake when it impacts their entire life. In Wolf City, they have contests to win the alpha's heart, where you compete with dozens of other women. He dates them all at the same time because of your curse. It's messed up."

Willow shook her head. "I would kill them all."

I grinned. This chick was going to be a good friend, I could tell.

Rab dropped his fork on the plate. "Okay, I get it, we messed up forever ago and there is a good reason city wolves hate us. Can we move on?"

I nodded, shoving a mouthful of yummy spiced beans into my mouth as a flavor explosion of cumin burst across my tongue. "Yes. Let's move on. I know you don't like me, but I'm all that you have left, so I'm just going to have to do." I shrugged.

Willow stilled. "Does that mean...you'll go to the Dark Woods and prove yourself as alpha?"

Her hand went to her belly and I sighed.

"Yes. You think I'm going to let your baby be born a human and eat dried beans and rice for the rest of their life? I told you, I'm here to help." Dammit, their entrapment had worked. I was going all in.

Rab looked me up and down then, scanning my body with the gaze of a predator as if looking for weak spots or wounds to exploit. "Run was the greatest alpha of our time, and it took him three years to find his way through the Dark Woods to the Cave of Magic. Do you really think you can even make it out of there alive?"

My wolf surged to the surface then and I glared

at him. "Have you ever had an alpha who was a split shifter?"

Willow lifted a finger. "Angel wolf, and no, we haven't," she agreed, and Rab shot her a glare.

"You're not trained," Rab said. "The first cold night, you'll lose your fingers to frostbite." He took a bite of rice and beans, chewing it slowly.

Okay, frostbite sounded bad, but after my time with Marmal and running through Dark Fey Territory, I was no longer scared of being alone in the wild. "Then teach me as much as you can in the next twenty-four hours, because I'm going and I'm coming back in three days with magic that will fix this land and save your people."

He looked at me like I was a puzzle he couldn't figure out. "Our."

I frowned. "Huh?"

"Our people, and if positive mental attitude could help you out there, I wouldn't worry so much."

I smiled, taking another bite of food.

"But it can't," he growled. "So be ready for a master class in woodland survival."

I gulped.

Was I really doing this? Going out alone into a place called the Dark Woods in order to find some magical cave and possibly get lost for *years*?

No, I couldn't think like that.

Seeing Willow stroke her pregnant belly longingly

though, I knew I had to try, and I could leave nothing to chance. Nothing.

"Willow, do you have a fancy dress I could borrow?" I asked.

CHAPTER FOUR

EUGENE SHOWED UP LATER THAT AFTERNOON AND I made him turn right back around and take me to Sawyer. That I was staying was something I had to tell him in person, and there was something I had to *do* in person too. I'd asked Astra to accompany us, as well as twenty guards. Surprisingly, Rab himself had volunteered to go. He and I had turned a corner, and I was grateful to no longer be butting heads with him.

"Why are we traipsing through war-torn woods with you all dressed up?" Eugene asked as he held a gun at his side, finger on the trigger.

I smoothed the red and gold silk handmade dress that Willow had given me. With the bright colors and the way it draped over one shoulder, it reminded me of an Indian sari. I'd tied up my hair into a sleek bun and used beetroot powders Willow had given me to stain my lips and cheeks.

It wasn't exactly what I had in mind for my wedding day look, but it would have to do.

"Because I'm going away for a while and I won't leave without being Sawyer's wife first," I said, determined. I wasn't going to go into some wild Dark Woods and let the curse kill my mate if I ended up gone for three years.

Eugene stopped dead and looked up at me, tears glistening in his eyes. "Does he know?"

I shook my head. "Not yet. I know he has a lot going on."

Eugene cleared his throat, straightening his shoulders and nodded. "I'll get you there and back safely. Don't worry."

He stepped in front of me with seemingly renewed strength as we continued our walk through the woods. I stumbled over ferns and small shrubs, holding up the edges of my dress to make my way over to Astra. We'd left the Paladin horses and donkeys in favor of going on foot. A troop of twenty warriors on horseback was loud; we could be stealthier this way.

"Astra?" I stepped next to her and she looked up at me with a smile. Always smiling at me this one, such an innocent and loving soul.

"Yes, Alpha?"

I'd long stopped asking her to call me that. "You're like a priest or a pastor, right?"

She frowned, looking confused.

"Like...you are an important person of God. You... marry people?" I hedged.

Her eyes widened as a grin broke out on her lips and she looked at my dress in a whole new light.

"Yes, Alpha, it would be my honor to oversee your joining union."

Joining union must be what they called a wedding. "Okay, great. Thanks."

We crept through the trees, and the once far-off noises of war grew closer and louder. Nothing new to see here, folks, just creeping through the war-ridden woods to surprise my fiancé with a wedding he knew nothing about.

'*Hey, we're like twenty minutes away. Are my parents and Raven still in the bunker?*' I asked.

I really wanted my dad to walk me down the aisle, but I wouldn't pull him from safety if things were still in a lockdown kind of situation.

'*Yes. Everyone who isn't fighting is down there. It's a secret bunker under the school...which has been completely shelled out.*'

I stumbled over my footing. Shelled out? My mind spun. '*What do you mean* shelled out?'

I felt the agitation run through him, but knew it wasn't meant to be directed at me. '*It's gone, Demi. Sterling Hill is completely gone, but the bunker holds strong. It's thirty feet underground, with twelve inches of steel and concrete, and they've got a two-year food supply down there.*'

Dizziness washed over me. Why would they need a two-year food supply? *'Sawyer, are they...trapped under there?'*

'Not trapped, but I've told them not to come out until we win the war.'

Until we win the war? My parents could be in an underground bunker for weeks? Or even months? My head swam with the thought of that. I was about to ask something else when a weird whistling sound cut through the air. A body tumbled over me and I was taken to the ground. Using my hands to break the fall, I hit the ground hard, landing the brunt of my weight on my palms. My gaze snapped to the man who'd thrown me to the ground, and a split second later a steel-tipped arrow sank into the soil beside me.

"Stay down," Rab barked, and then popped up to his knees, pulling an arrow from the quiver at his back so quickly I could barely track his movements. Within seconds, he loosed the arrow into the top of a tree, and then a body fell from it, hitting the ground with a thud.

Holy rattlesnake.

My heart hammered in my chest as I stared at the dead figure on the ground. Shrill yelps rang out in the woods, and then footsteps could be heard as a group of people retreated.

Rab and his men pulled their weapons and formed a semicircle in front of me as Astra and Eugene fell to the ground at my left and right side. I sat up, brushing the dirt off of the dress Willow had loaned me. Rab inched forward, inspecting the body at the base of the tree.

That was close, I thought, as I stared at the arrow that had been inches from my neck.

Eugene pulled his gun and aimed it at the thick outcrop of trees to the left, while Astra bowed her head in prayer and clasped her hands, mumbling under her breath.

"Ithaki! They've retreated!" Rab called from the base of the tree.

"That was too close for my liking," Eugene said, and hauled me up by the armpit, tucking me into his body.

"You and me both," I told him as I steadied myself.

Astra ceased praying. Her eyes popped open and she just stared at her clasped hands like they held some horror. "They shot an arrow into our territory..." Her voice held fear.

Rab and his men sauntered over, all of them frowning.

"Maybe it was a mistake," one of the men said.

Rab reached down and gently pulled Astra to her feet, looking at her like a beloved sister.

Her voice was small: "It wasn't a mistake."

Rab met my eyes and I saw fear in his for the first time. "It was an act of war," he declared.

My heart sank into my stomach like a stone. How many wars could we handle at one time? Was this my fault? The Ithaki and Paladin peoples had a long peace between them, and I'd gone and brought war. Guilt gnawed at me as I pondered this, but it quickly turned to anger.

How dare they? How dare the Ithaki try to pick us off when they probably knew we were weak?

I stood angrily, brushing off my dress, glaring at the woods before turning to the line of twenty men. They held bows as if anticipating another hit. "The next time a twig so much as snaps, you shoot in that direction!" I ordered them.

"Yes, Alpha," a few of the men said in unison.

Rab's eyes went wide as he looked from the men to me. "*That* title is earned."

The men who'd said it lowered their heads in shame. "Yes, sir."

Why was he always against me? This situation was hard enough without him pushing my face into the mud. So much for our friendly ways. He was Rabid once more.

"And I intend to earn it!" I snapped at Rab, turning on my heel and stalking off to marry the love of my life before I went on a suicide mission for my people.

———·——

Twenty minutes later, the earsplitting sounds of gunfire and magic crackling boomed through the air. A distinctive smell lingered. Gunpowder and hot wires, copper and blood.

'I'm here, at the bord—'

"Demi!" Sawyer whisper-screamed nearby. Elation bubbled up in my chest and then spilled over into my limbs at the sound of his voice. I burst into a run and broke out of the woods, cleared the small stone fence and orange flags, and ran to him. He was surrounded by over fifty armed men. Most of them were city wolves with guns and knives, but about a dozen were Paladins. They held vicious-looking spears and stared out into the woods with sharp gazes. I noticed Sage among them, her bright red hair tied up into a tight topknot as she held two guns at her sides and whispered to Walsh beside her.

I ran in my dress, somehow not tripping over anything, and Sawyer stood atop the hill and opened his arms. I jumped into them and they tightened around me. The second his earthy scent hit my nostrils, my throat tightened with emotion and I breathed him in.

Mate. Pack. Home.

'*I missed you so much,*' I whimpered through our imprint. His feelings mixed with mine and I sifted through each one. Love, protection, anxiety, trepidation, loyalty.

"We can't stay out here, sir. We're too exposed." I recognized that voice as the army commander dude who I had met briefly before.

Sawyer kept his arms tightly around me, and turned to walk away as I watched over his shoulder while he carried me, refusing to let me go. Rab and his men lined up with the Paladins who had volunteered to protect

Wolf City, and I noticed Arrow and his brother give each other curt nods before they whispered under their breath.

Rab was probably telling his little brother about the Ithaki all but declaring war with their attack on us.

"You shouldn't have come," Sawyer whispered in my ear as he held me tightly to his chest and walked us both up the hill to a building I didn't recognize. "It's too dangerous for you, my love." When we reached the top, he finally slid me down his body so that I could stand.

"Why are you wearing that dress?" He looked confused as he fully took me in. I'm sure he didn't know it was a Paladin wedding dress, but it was a fancy dress and not ideal for traipsing through the woods. My knees were stained with dirt too. Not my Pinterest wedding look.

"Sawyer, I—"

"We need to get you inside." The Commander used his body to shepherd Sawyer and me toward the building. Sage slipped next to me and gave me a quick side hug before moving back into the line of warriors around us.

I looked up at the building, perplexed. It was a single-level brick building that looked like it was used for industrial purposes, like a water treatment plant or something. It was not where I imagined Sawyer hiding out. As we neared a tall chain-link fence that glowed with a magical green hue, I saw two figures standing at either side of the opening.

Witches.

They came. My idea worked!

Sawyer seemed to know what I was thinking. '*We are now officially taking witch and warlock refugees in exchange for service to the war. It was a brilliant idea, Demi.*'

The witches saw Sawyer approaching and snapped their fingers, causing an opening to form in the protective green bubble. We stepped through and I frowned as I noticed the dilapidated state the building was in. "What about your parents' house? Is this where you're stationed now?"

The concrete walls were stained with red rust that ran in thin rivulets down the dusty gray slabs. The roof was patched with a blue tarp and looked like it would cave in at any moment. This surely wasn't where the alpha of Werewolf City commanded a war.

Sawyer met the Commander's gaze and something passed between them before he sighed to me. "My parents' house is gone, Demi. The opposition is going after well-known places. This one is safer. We move every twelve hours."

My legs gave out then and Sawyer caught me. His house was gone; the school was gone... I'd only been away for a day and it seemed the entire city was falling to enemy hands. "Your mother?" I gasped.

"She's fine. We got her out and into the bunker with everyone else." Sawyer's voice was devoid of any emotion.

Shock ripped through me. My parents were in a bunker; the school was gone; Sawyer's parents' house was gone.

"Why did you come, Demi? What did you need to tell me? I'm almost scared to ask." Sawyer's voice was low as we stood just under the entryway of the broken building.

My throat seized up, unable to say the words, unable to find my strength. Everyone else was inside of the fenced area but giving us privacy. Still...a few would hear.

'Demi, you're scaring me, love, and I'm not sure how much more I can take.'

A tear slid down my cheek. "Sawyer, the Paladins are...they're in rough shape. Their crops have a black fungus and the land is dying. On top of that, their children being born are *human*. All because they don't have an acting alpha."

Sawyer's eyes widened. "Human? What do you mean?"

"They aren't like city wolves. Their wolf is more tied to alpha magic and the land than it is to genetics, I guess. I don't understand it all. I just know that I can't turn my back on them. They are a beautiful people."

Sawyer rubbed his temples and nodded. "Okay. Alright, we will figure it out. You can be their alpha and I'll be the Werewolf City alpha, and I'll build a fucking mansion right on the center line of our two lands if I have to, Demi. Whatever you need. Whatever it takes to keep us together."

The sob I had been keeping inside ripped from my throat then and Sawyer frowned, reaching for me.

"I thought that was a good thing to say? Why are you crying?" The poor guy looked so confused, I knew I just needed to come out with it. He was so fucking perfect and he didn't even know.

"Sawyer, I can't just declare myself their alpha like you can. I have to earn it," I told him.

He went very still then, eyes thinning to slits. "How?" His voice was thick with his wolf and I knew what he was thinking: a barbaric dominance fight, but it was so much worse than that.

I swallowed hard. "I need to go away for a few days…maybe longer. I need to go into the Dark Woods and—"

"The Dark Woods!" he shouted, and half the warriors nearest us turned to stare, open-mouthed.

I pulled him deeper into the overhang of the roof, leaning against the wall of the building as the low, flickering light cast macabre shadows over Sawyer's face. The scent of mildew surrounded us and I almost wanted to cry. This was so not the glamourous wedding day I wanted. "Once I'm in the Dark Woods, I have to find some magic cave. Alone. Only then can I return as alpha."

Sawyer tipped his head back and laughed, a deep

throaty laugh that was full of sarcasm. "Send my future wife into the Dark Woods alone? Over my *dead fucking body*, Demi."

I sighed. I knew it would be another fight, and I was prepared for that, but he hadn't even heard the worst of it.

"Sawyer, it's normally a three-day trip…" I chewed my lip and his chiseled jaw clenched.

"Normally?" His piercing blue eyes thinned to slits.

"It took my biological father three years. The woods trick you and only reveal the cave when you are ready or something. That's why I came in person to see you. I don't want to leave anything up to chance." I grasped his hand, pleased to see he was still wearing his father's wedding ring, which I'd placed on his finger before I left. "Marry me? Tonight. Right now? It will ensure that if I get lost, the curse won't take you or your mom or Sage or anyone you love."

He stared at me…frozen, eyes wide. "You're serious? That's why you wore the dress? Demi…" He pulled his hand from mine and massaged his chest as if he were feeling physical pain. "I can't let you go into the Dark Woods alone if that's what you're asking."

Here we go.

"I'm not asking," I said, my throat tightening to the point of pain as I swallowed my sobs. "I'm going with or without your permission, Sawyer. I'm asking you to make me your wife tonight so I don't have to worry about you while I'm out there."

His head reeled back in shock. "Demi, three years. You said three years."

I grabbed the sides of his face. "No. That was Run. It won't be me. I'll be back in three days, a week tops. I will *not* get lost."

His chest heaved as he stared into my eyes. "What if, after we win the war, we invited all of the Paladin to live here. We can feed them and—"

"The babies, Sawyer, they're being born human, without magic. And soon the people will follow."

He frowned. "I mean, being human isn't the worst thing—"

I scoffed. "Okay, let's rip your wolf away from you and see how you feel."

He winced. "You're right, it's awful, but, Demi...the Dark Woods...alone."

"Sawyer, I know you think I'm fragile, but I'm not. I can do this." I squared my shoulders in grim determination and Sawyer's lips quirked.

"My love, you're about as fragile as a bomb."

I chuckled. "I need that on a T-shirt."

Sawyer laced his fingers through mine and then looked down at his foot, hiking up his pantleg to show me the ankle monitor. It was glowing a sickly green. "I can't follow you, babe. As much as I would want to go with you, I couldn't. The witches have been able to keep them from tracking me with this, but they can't get it off."

And even if he could, he wasn't allowed. Plus we were at war; he had to be there for his people.

I nodded.

"You sure you want to do this? Go into the Dark Woods alone and prove yourself as a Paladin alpha? All of it?"

I thought of all the people I had met today, and of the sweet man, Red Moon, my grandfather, who'd stepped over the line into Ithaki land to help me. I thought of Willow rubbing her belly, and imagined her having a child born without a wolf, without magic. I thought of the dying crops and the beautiful village they'd built only to see it eaten away by the black fungus. But most of all, I thought of the small thrill of pride that rushed through me when Astra looked into my eyes with absolute conviction and called me Alpha.

"Yes. I have to."

A sadness crossed his face, before it was quickly replaced with a half-cocked smile. "Then let's get married."

———•·•———

Ten minutes later, Sage walked down our makeshift aisle holding a bunch of wildflowers under the darkening sky as the moonlight shone down on us. Walsh stood next to Sawyer in the open grass field of the industrial building, and armed warriors and witches made a circle of protection around us. It wasn't pretty, but it still felt special.

"Ready, dear?" Eugene asked, extending his arm to me.

I nodded, trying to keep from crying. My dad was deep in a bunker with my mom underground, and Eugene had graciously offered to give me away. As I walked slowly toward Sawyer, he held my gaze with a loving intensity I wasn't sure I deserved. I was reminded in this moment of the first time I met him, standing there at Delphi, while Astra stood patiently in the center and waited for us to reach her. In her hands was a small leather-bound book; the cover was decorated with a cluster of deep red stones; it was something spiritual, I was sure. It was small enough to fit in her pocket, and I wondered if she always carried it. When I reached Sawyer, he shook Eugene's hand and then took my right hand in his, walking me over to where Astra stood.

I didn't know how the curse worked, but Sawyer had informed Astra about what words needed to be said to test the curse. If I didn't truly love Sawyer, he would die on the spot. I wasn't worried. I'd never loved anyone more than I loved this man.

Even now, after I'd just told him I didn't need his permission to go off into the woods for an undetermined amount of time and we'd argued, he still looked at me like I was the love of his life. I wished I had my camera to capture all of Sawyer's looks, because this one, it was so tender, so endearing, I wanted to memorize it forever. I brushed my finger over his knuckles and he grinned.

Astra took our clasped hands in hers and then bowed her head. "Dear Father, thank you for bringing these two souls together in the name of true love. May they be blessed in all that they do together. May they be quick to love and slow to anger. May their children be healthy and carefree and may their love only deepen over time."

She looked up from her prayer at me and I had to blink back tears. Sawyer looked misty-eyed as well. It was perfect. The perfect thing to say.

"Is there anything you would like to say before I read the curse-testing spell?" Astra asked us.

I nodded, turning to Sawyer. "Sawyer, I think the thing I love most about you is how you love me." He grinned and I went on. "You support everything I want to do, even if it drives you up a wall, and that speaks volumes about your character and the kind of man and leader you are. And you're not awful to look at either."

His grin grew wider as Sage, Walsh, and those listening chuckled.

"I just hope that I can be worthy of that kind of pure love. My wish is to be your equal and continue to push our love to the edges of the universe over the years as we grow old together."

I looked at Astra to indicate that I was done.

Astra smiled. "Sawyer?"

Sawyer nodded, his dark locks falling into his eyes as he did. "Demi, I am helpless to do anything but support you even when your ideas are driving me up a wall." Everyone chuckled. "There is no world where I would deny you anything, even my own beating heart. You fulfill this need in me that I didn't even know I had. You were the glue that mended a tear that I wasn't aware was there until the moment I laid eyes on you."

Tears softly rolled down my cheeks as he let my hands go and cupped my chin, his gaze burning into the very depths of my soul.

"I promise to continue to love you with an intensity that matches this fierce protectiveness I feel over you. I will protect you, your dreams, and our future family with every fiber of my being, both as man and wolf." His eyes flashed yellow at that, and I leaned my forehead against his, letting the tears fall down my face.

Astra cleared her throat. "Demi Calloway and Sawyer Hudson, do you both wish to take the other as your lawful spouse and true mate?" Her voice was thick with emotion.

"I do," Sawyer and I said in unison.

Astra nodded, pulling a folded piece of parchment from the top of her book. I had seen Sawyer handing it to her earlier and knew the curse was about to be tested.

Bring it on.

"Then I test this curse on the Hudson family," Astra said loudly for all surrounding us to hear, "and declare you both as man and wife. Sawyer, you may kiss your bride." Astra folded the paper and looked at us expectantly.

My heart hammered in my ears as the smell of hot wires filtered through the air.

Magic.

Sawyer's face lit up with an orangish glow as his skin seemed to radiate like the sun. I could feel the heat from here as he leaned into me. Did he fear kissing me? Testing this curse? Or did he know as assuredly as I did that my love for him was true?

As if in answer to my internal question, he reached up with confidence and grasped the sides of my face, pulling my mouth to meet his. Our lips touched and the searing heat of Sawyer's skin pierced right through me, sending an electric jolt down my spine and into my toes. There was a popping noise, and then everything went black.

CHAPTER FIVE

D EMI!" SAWYER SHOOK ME AS I PEERED UP AT HIM from the ground. A high-pitched whine rang in my ears as I shook my head. Sawyer's skin was covered in black soot like he'd been burned.

"Were we bombed?" I looked around, but everyone else seemed fine. In fact, they were all staring at us with furrowed brows.

Oh God. The curse.

"Are you dead?" I queried. Had I somehow killed us both?

Sawyer hauled me up to a standing position and glared at one of the defector witches, who had stepped over to help us.

"What happened?" he growled. "She loves me. I know it. Our love is *true*."

The witch sniffed the air and at the same time I smelled it too. Sulphur and...something sour, like curdled milk.

"Broken curse..." the witch mumbled.

"What?" Sawyer pressed her.

She shook her head. "I know that smell. It's the smell of a *broken* curse."

Sawyer and I looked at each other, dumbfounded. Was breaking the curse even an option?

He must have clued Sage in, because she didn't look confused about why we were talking about curses.

"Of course!" Sage snapped her fingers. "A city wolf alpha just married a half Paladin. Surely that would break a curse meant to tear apart our two packs?"

Astra threw her arms up to the sky. "Praise the Father!" she yelled, and in that moment a tiny sprinkle of rain fell from the sky. At first I thought she'd spit on me with her yelling, but slowly, a misty rain started to fall over us.

Sawyer grinned and then laughed. "It's broken? Our children won't have to worry?" His arms came around me and then I was hauled into the air as he spun me in a circle. Who knew that our love would be strong enough to break a centuries-old curse?

The warriors erupted into quiet cheers, and for a second I forgot about the war, about the fact that in a little while I needed to go away and leave Sawyer. Instead, I just let this be my wedding day and I reveled in the happiness of this moment.

Then a bomb went off. Literally. The air cracked with a loud boom as the ground shook, and Sawyer tucked me into him, throwing his body over mine protectively. A nearby tree ripped from the ground just outside the fence as light flared in the small space and clods of dirt were thrown into our group.

They missed hitting us. The witches' fence seemed to have held, but I wasn't going to bank on it a second time.

"We need to move!" the Commander screamed, and everyone scrambled, running into the building and coming out with duffel bags and equipment.

Sage tossed her bouquet on the ground and picked up a gun as the captain stepped over to Sawyer's side. Rab and Astra and the men I had brought fanned out behind me, waiting for my direction.

"Sir," the Commander said, "I think it's time to initiate plan B. They are on us and we've lost too many men."

Sawyer frowned. "I'm not ready to give up, hand them our territory, our homes, our farms on a silver platter."

The Commander looked at me. "Maybe if she were to give herself up, we could—"

"Shut up!" Sawyer launched forward and clasped his hand around the dude's mouth.

I frowned. What the hell was he doing, and what did the guy mean *give* myself up? Sawyer was the one wanted for murder. Sawyer was the one who started this whole war.

The soldiers nearest them stepped in to break them apart, prying Sawyer off the Commander. "At least tell her!" the Commander yelled. "Tell her this is all because of her. That she could stop it."

Sawyer's eyes narrowed just as mine widened. "You're relieved of duty, Commander. Get the fuck out of my face and into a bunker."

The man looked shocked. "Sir?"

"Go," Sawyer growled, pelts of fur rolling down his neck.

"What the hell is he talking about, Sawyer?" I yanked on my new husband's shirt and forced him to look at me.

I felt it then, between us, a deep dark secret he'd been keeping from me. It was thick and heavy and hidden deep within him.

"Sawyer, you tell me right now. I will not start our marriage off on lies," I growled at my mate.

He nodded, swallowing hard. "The others have formed the Magical Creatures Coalition. They will stop the war if I give into their demand. Just one demand."

Chills ran the length of my arms. "What's their demand?"

His gaze went to my feet then, unable to meet my eyes.

"Sawyer, what are they demanding?"

He shook his head like he couldn't speak.

"You," Sage said suddenly, and a wave of dizziness crashed into me.

"Me?"

Sawyer looked up from the ground and I came face-to-face with his wolf. Yellow glowing eyes stared back at me from behind his thick lashes. "This whole murder trial about Vicon was to get me out of the picture. They want your power, Demi. They want to bottle and sell what you have and become invincible, unkillable, the Fountain of Youth, whatever you want to call it. They want it."

Me?

They wanted me...

I'd known that the vampire queen wanted my power. I guess the fey too, but...to start a war over it... "All of them? Why?"

Sawyer's eyes flashed back to their searing blue. "Yes, all of them, and because, Demi"—he inhaled through his nose—"you're like a drug. Do you remember that first time we kissed? The vibrating?"

I nodded, remembering when he'd backed me up against the wall in the hallway of the Fine Arts building.

Sawyer swallowed hard, chewing at his lip nervously. "I took a bit of your power then, unknowingly. I was so strong, so fast after that kiss, I felt...invincible. Every time we have been close after that, I've had to be very careful not to..."

Horror ripped through me at his words. He *took* my power? He had to be careful not to what? Drain me like a vampire?!

"Not to?" I needed to hear him say it.

"Not to consume your essence, not to take from you."

My mind was spinning, this entire war...wasn't over Sawyer killing Vicon... It was over *me*.

It was...sick and wrong and...I couldn't let all of these people die because of me. I couldn't let buildings burn and our people lose everything they had over one person.

"I'll go," I told him. "Give myself up, and later, when our army is stronger, you can get me back."

"No!" Sawyer growled as fur rippled from his neck to his arms.

The Paladin people would have to wait. I couldn't let thousands die because I refused to give myself up. "Sawyer, I will not be known for this. I will *not* be a coward. I will do what is right," I said boldly, tipping my chin high.

He looked at someone behind me and nodded quickly, and then I felt two strong arms pin my wrists behind my back. "Sorry, love," Eugene breathed in my ear.

Panic flooded my system as I realized Sawyer would never let me turn myself in.

"Sawyer! Be reasonable. This *entire city* will fall! I will *not* have blood on my hands," I wept.

I jerked against Eugene as he started to drag me backward. It was not lost on me that this was probably my karma for having Sawyer held against his will while I left.

"It will be on *my* hands," Sawyer growled, "and this entire city will fall before I let one hair on your head be harmed. Demi, you can't let them have your power or we will be dealing with a whole new monster altogether." He rushed forward and kissed me chastely before backing away. "I love you. Go back to the Paladin lands, where you are safe. They won't look for you there."

The shock that rushed through my system then was too much and I felt my wolf come to the surface. "Sawyer, no! Just let me—"

Something pricked the side of my neck and I turned to follow the direction it came from.

Rab.

He was holding a fucking blow dart. But instead of looking malicious or greedy, he looked brokenhearted. "I will make sure she gets back to Paladin Village, and I will send every spare man I have to help you win the war," Rab told Sawyer, and placed his fist over his chest.

Dizziness took hold of me, the trees started to blur behind him, and it felt like I had suddenly been thrown into a washing machine.

"No! I can't!" I screamed, but it was warbled, like I was talking underwater.

"Thank you. That would be much appreciated,"

Sawyer told Rab. His voice was so deep it made me laugh. I giggled in a low whalelike tone, and then sagged in Eugene's arms as I lost consciousness.

———··———

I came to with a foggy memory of what had transpired. Why was I being carried and why was the person carrying me running? Then it hit me.

Sawyer. The war. It was all my fault.

"No, take me back!" My voice croaked as I pounded on Eugene's back. My rib cage slammed into his shoulder with each step he took. He had me in a fireman hold and was running so fast I felt dizzy. A loud bang ripped throughout the space and I jerked my head back to see Sage and Walsh running behind Eugene through the dense forest. Their arms were outstretched as they shot into the darkened trees with sleek black guns. Bursts of light fired from the muzzles as adrenaline rushed through my system and I felt more alert. Arrows rained down around us, sticking into the wet ground with thunks as Rab and his men created a tight circle around me.

"Astra!" I yelped, my eyes scanning for the young girl.

"I'm here, Alpha!" she said to my right, running balls-out, her short-cropped hair bouncing behind her. Rab put a horn of some type to his lips and blew, loudly.

The deep horn resonated inside my body. My entire head felt like it was going to explode.

Another horn responded off in the distance and Rab yelped out in relief.

'War horn. The village will be ready to defend against the oncoming attack,' Astra told me as they ran.

My head was still foggy, but it was clear that someone was chasing us. Vampires didn't use bows and arrows, so it must be fey or Ithaki. I was just wondering which when an ultrasonic pitch slammed into my ears and Eugene stumbled.

That was a fey calling card, and if it was bows and arrows, my guess was dark fey or Ithaki. Or both.

"Put me down, I can run," I told Eugene, and he obliged, letting me fall to my feet before he covered his ears.

Without a second thought, I let my wolf free. I wasn't going to let this fey weaken our group and then take us out one by one. No way.

My wolf was semitransparent one second and then solid the next. 'Find the screamer and rip their throat out,' I told her.

"Rab! Cover my wolf!" I then barked to the Paladin leader, screaming so that my voice could be heard over the shrill noise.

We'd stopped, and everyone covered their ears as the trees rustled and my legs went weak with the effects of the fey noise weapon. My brain felt like it was being put into a blender.

I winced as I watched my wolf take off into the trees

and Rab and his men ran with her, shooting arrows left and right. I blinked, and then I was looking out from her perspective. My wolf—she smelled him.

Ithaki. Fey-warlock. A deadly combination.

My wolf's head was low to the ground, ears flattened as she locked in on where the noise was coming from. Cutting to the right, she took off faster than Rab and his boys could follow. Trees passed in dark blurs as her paws pounded the damp, packed earth. As she neared the fey Ithaki, my entire head felt like it was going to explode both in human and wolf form. He was hiding behind a thick tree trunk, and my wolf howled as she leaped. The earsplitting ultrasonic sound cut off with a yelp as her teeth sank into his neck.

I snapped my attention back to my human form and the half dozen warriors surrounding me. "Be ready for anything," I told them. My wolf had just taken out the Ithaki's precious brain melting sonic howler; there would be repercussions. The trees rustled as a blur of a figure zoomed toward us.

Vampire Ithaki.

I rushed forward, using my own freaky super speed, and met the figure halfway. We crashed into each other and I suddenly came face-to-face with a snarling male. His ears were pointed like a fey's but his teeth distended like a vampire's. It was freaky and he needed to die immediately. With a furious growl, I made a fist and slammed it into his throat until I heard the crunching of bone.

I followed up with a knee to the groin as his wrist snaked out and grasped me by the throat. Rage flooded through me. I could simultaneously feel my wolf ripping into the Ithaki fey as I felt this vampire try to kill me.

Enough is enough.

We had too many wars going on, and I still had to go into the Dark Woods and prove myself as a Paladin alpha. There was no time for this bullshit. Reeling my head back, I headbutted his nose with surprising force. The sharp crack splintered the air and my head throbbed. But the move worked; he let up on my windpipe, so I went for the kill. Reaching up, I took his head into my hands and cradled his jaw with my fingers. One swift crack to the left and I snapped his neck. He fell to the ground in a heap.

I'd heard stories about vampires reawakening after a broken neck or bad accident. I wasn't leaving that to chance. Sage appeared on my right just in time; she came down hard on the center of his chest with a silver stake. The hollow thud made chills rush up my spine as his skin started to crumble into black ash.

My wolf trotted over to me, looking pleased with her kill, and the sound of the Ithakis' retreating footsteps was music to my ears.

"Well done." Rab appraised the dead vampire and I noticed his spear was dripping with purple Ithaki blood.

I frowned. "They'll be back with more I'm sure."

How had things gotten so bad so fast? This was one hell of a honeymoon.

"Come on." Rab, Eugene, and Walsh tucked Astra in the center of their little circle next to me and we jogged the rest of the way to the Paladin village.

Using our imprint, I felt for my mate, weaving my energy into Sawyer as my wolf jogged alongside me. I sensed he was busy and in danger. Spikes of anger, confusion, and fear weaved from him and then seeped into me.

Not a good time to check in…

As we neared the trail of lights that led to the Paladin village, Rab pulled the horn to his lips and blew two short bursts. Immediately, two short bursts were returned. We came out of the thick trees and my eyes widened at the sight before me. The entire wall of the village was filled with Paladin warriors. Male, female, young, old. They crouched on the edge of the wall wearing blue face paint and menacing scowls. They held daggers, spears, and arrows that gleamed with a sickly green poison tip.

Pride swelled in my chest, and I couldn't help the grin that spread across my face. The Paladin people were like one cohesive unit, ready to defend their land at all costs.

I didn't know Run…I didn't even get to know Red, but in a way I felt like I did know them. Through these people, I got to know them, and it was going to be an honor to serve as their alpha—assuming that was something I was "found worthy" to do.

As if she heard my thoughts, Astra slipped her hand into mine. "I will prepare the alpha trial ceremony. You will leave at first light to the Dark Woods."

I'd considered turning myself in to the vampires for half a second but that wasn't a guarantee to stop the war and it would still leave a huge problem here with no one to fix it. I gulped as nerves filtered through me, but then I saw the fierce determination and courage of the Paladin people crouched on the wall, ready to defend their land and their families, and I swallowed my fear down. "It would be my honor."

Some things were bigger than you and that was scary. What if I died out in the Dark Woods? What if I took five years to get back here and Sawyer remarried? There were so many what-ifs that my head swam, but I focused on the only ones I wanted to. What if I made it in and out quickly; what if I saved an entire race of people and their land? What if I became a worthy alpha of the Paladin people? Those what-ifs circled my head all night until I fell asleep.

CHAPTER SIX

I WAS AWOKEN BY THE SMELL OF SMOKE. THE SCENT of sage hit my nostrils, making my eyes fly open. Astra was walking around my room in the guest-house fanning the smoke over everything. I inhaled. Something sickeningly sweet and earthy was mixed with the sage. I groaned as the last remnants of sleep left me. Astra ignored me, mumbling prayers lightly under her breath.

"What is that?" I peered at the small gray marble bowl she held. It was still dark out, the sun barely coming up as a faint glow filtered through the curtains.

"Sage and frankincense," she said quickly before going back to mumbling her prayers.

"Knock, knock." Rab's voice came from the hallway, and I held my arms over my braless chest. I was wearing a thin white T-shirt and not ready for company.

"Come in." I guess it was a party in my bedroom at the butt crack of dawn.

Rab stepped in with Sage right behind him. She wore her hair in a topknot and looked super alert and awake. How long had I slept? By the feel of my heavy skin, it was not long.

Why the hell was everyone so perky?

Sage pointed at Rab's ass and mouthed, *"Yum,"* causing me to grin.

I would have to break it to her later that he was married.

"You have two hours until the alpha trial ceremony," Rab said. "I wanted to take that time to give you some bushcraft skills and local plant knowledge to help you survive in the woods."

And buzzkill. Way to remind me of my possible impending doom.

But there was some relief at his words. This city girl going off into the woods alone could very much use some knowledge of the land. "Thank you, that would be awesome. I'll be right out."

He nodded curtly and turned to leave before stopping. "Eat a big breakfast. You don't know when you'll have your next meal."

Then he left.

You don't know when you'll have your next meal! That was the most horrifying thing anyone had ever said to me.

"He's such an angry ball of yum," Sage purred as she watched Rab head down the hall and I popped out of bed to get dressed.

"He's married. Wife is preggo and super cool."

Sage scowled. "Dammit."

Astra hissed, and it took me a minute to realize why.

"Don't cuss," I told Sage.

My redheaded bestie rolled her eyes, and I couldn't help but think of Raven in that moment. Raven and Sage would be like two peas in a pod, they were so similar. I hoped she was still safe in the bunker with my parents.

I put on breathable cargo pants and a sports bra, a loose top, and Nike tennis shoes Sage had brought me. My official Dark Woods hiking attire was complete with a bandana around my neck.

"What's up with you and Walsh?" If she was all over Rab, things couldn't be good.

She frowned. "Nothing. We're...nothing. He wants to focus on the war and...it's whatever." Her eyes glistened with tears and my heart sank into my stomach. Walsh was such a douchebag. Why did he keep playing hot and cold with her?

"Oh, girl, I'm so sorry." I opened my arms and went to hug her when she put her hands out.

"No hugs! It makes it worse. Everyone knows that. I'm fine. Let's feed you." She turned on her heel and spun out of the room.

I frowned. Watching my best friend go through

something painful right when I was about to leave made me sad. Hopefully, when I got back, we could all go into the bunker together with Raven and support each other through this war. I just needed to push everything else out of my mind for the time being and focus on one thing.

The alpha trial.

Astra kept praying and waving smoke around me as I ran a brush through my hair and then tied it into a long thick braid at my back.

"So two hours and then I meet you across the street?" I asked her.

She nodded, never ceasing her mumbling as she wafted smoke into my face, causing me to cough and sputter.

Twenty minutes later, I felt like I was going to puke, I was so full. Apparently Sage had woken up early and cooked me a farewell feast. She'd taken powdered eggs, black beans, rice, and shoved them all into a homemade burrito with fresh ground-corn tortillas. I'd eaten two of those and promptly regretted the second one.

After chugging water, I met Rab outside where he waited on the porch watching the sun come up.

"How good of a student are you? Can you retain lots of information fairly quickly?" He pushed off the wall he'd been leaning on and I shrugged.

"Yeah, decent. I mean, can I take notes?" Shit, this was starting to stress me out. Would there be a quiz?

He shook his head. "You can't bring anything into the Dark Woods but the clothes on your back. No weapons, no food, nothing. You must prove that you can become one with nature and live off the land. You must be strong enough for the magic to choose you so that you can lead our people."

I gulped. "Okay. Yeah, no biggie. Hit me with knowledge."

He nodded and started to walk, so I followed him. "The first thing you'll want to do is locate water. Then you'll want to make a weapon. Multiple weapons. Spears, small knives, big knives, arrows, everything you can. Using one of the knives you make, you can kill an animal for its meat and later skin the hide to use for a bedroll, or most importantly a water canteen." He pulled something off his belt and handed it to me.

It was a suede water bladder sewn with a needle and thread. "Study how it's made so you can do it again," he told me.

My eyes bugged out as what he said overwhelmed me. We were thirty freaking seconds into this lesson, and I was already on information overload. "I can't bring a water bottle!?"

He shook his head. "No."

"Well, then I'm screwed," I declared. "I doubt there will be a needle and thread lying around so—"

"Bone, or even deer antlers. It's very brittle. If you chisel away at it with your knife, you can make a needle.

Also, some wooden sticks can be used as needles. Thread from your clothes or hemp or intestines of an animal—"

An involuntary whimper escaped my throat and Rab turned to me, placing one hand on each of my shoulders. His hard blue eyes peered deeply into my soul as I felt myself actually disappointing him in that moment. It was the heavy, sick feeling of total failure.

"You think I want this to be you?" he snapped, gripping my shoulders tightly. "I wish it could be me. You're the last person who should be going out into the Dark Woods and asking our ancestors to bless you with magic for our people." His face looked pained, like he might actually cry. "Alpha children train their entire lives for the trials, and unfortunately you missed out on that, but the time for weakness has passed. You need to dig deep inside of yourself and find whatever strength you have left. You *have* to take this seriously."

I swallowed hard, yanking myself out of his grasp. "I am! But Astra said it's only a three-day walk there and back. I can find water, drink it, and be back before I need to make a canteen from the kidney of a cow or whatever."

He scoffed. "That kind of thinking will get you killed. The second you step foot in the Dark Woods, you need to treat it like your new home, like you could be there forever."

Forever.

"I refuse to do that." I crossed my arms in defiance, my wolf coming to the surface to glare at him.

I could hear his teeth clamp shut from here. "Then our land dies, our magic dies, and our women go barren. *You* kill the magic growing inside of my child."

I staggered backward as if his words had physically reached out and slapped me.

"Never mind. You're a lost cause." He huffed and turned to leave.

Shit. Shit. Shit.

He'd gotten up at the ass crack of dawn to teach me how to survive and here I was being a bitch to him.

"Wait, Rab. I'm sorry." I ran to catch up with him. "You're right. I need to learn all of this in case I am there longer than the few days I have planned. I'm just...I'm scared, okay? But I am strong; I am ready for this. *Please* teach me."

He stopped, looking back at me behind a mess of brown hair.

With a sigh, he turned and pointed to a familiar white root sticking out of the ground. "That's ch—"

"Cholka root. Pain reliever," I told him.

He appraised me with pride. "Maybe there's hope for you yet, city girl."

Over the next two hours he showed me which plants and roots and berries were edible and which ones I could rub on the tip of my dart for poison. He went over basic wound care, such as using sunlight to help heal, always using clean water to wash the wound, and he taught me how to make a paste that involved an antibacterial moss and cholka root.

He told me about how to make homemade sunscreen out of clay, and in the end he even showed me how to skin and gut a rabbit.

I only cried three times and threw up once.

I longed for my iPhone, Range Rover, and Instagram then, but knew those days were long behind me.

At the end of the lesson, with only fifteen minutes left, he taught me how to make fire. I'd been rolling the damn stick between my fingers for what seemed like forever. I leaned forward holding the other stick and kindling with my feet, and did some crazy yoga-type pose so that I could also blow softly on the sparks that were coming from the sticks rubbing together.

My palms had heated up more than the sticks at this point. "Ughhh, this is too hard. I'll figure it out later." I stopped rubbing my hands and looked up at Rab, my not-so-patient teacher.

He consulted his watch. "You have three more minutes, and giving up isn't an option. Keep going. Fire is one of the most important things you can learn to make. Water, fire, food, shelter," he said, repeating his little lesson.

With a growl, I started rubbing my hands together, faster this time, vampire fast.

"Come on, you little shits!" I screamed at the wood

as sparks flew into the kindling and I huffed slowly. A small tendril of smoke started to wind up the stick and excitement thrummed through me.

Yes! Come on, baby!

I blew harder, and then orange flames flared to life below my palms, causing a yelp of pride to rip from my throat. I looked up at Rab with a giant grin to find him scowling at me with crossed arms.

He shrugged. "Well, I've done all I can. Hopefully, you make it back."

Grumpy ass.

The grin fell from my face and I was about to retort when a loud drum beat from the center of town.

Rab sighed, exhaling deeply before opening his palms to me. "The alpha trial has begun."

I swallowed hard, standing, and we both walked toward the church building to the sound of beating drums.

Whether it was a good time or not, I needed to check in with Sawyer.

'Sawyer? I'm going to be heading out in a few minutes. Hopefully we can still talk while I'm there, but…just in case…how are things there?'

I felt his anxiety through our bond. *'Hey, love. Sorry I had to have them take you away like that. Being in the Paladin lands right now is best for you. It's getting bad here.'*

I understood why he had to do what he did even

if I didn't like it. From my short amount of time being kidnapped by the vampires, I could see their dark plans for me, and I had no intention of allowing them to do that. Like Sawyer said, we'd be dealing with an entirely different beast altogether.

'How bad is it there?'

He paused. I could feel him wanting to hide whatever this was from me. *'Sawyer, how bad?'*

'We're losing, Demi. At some point, I need to choose between letting all of my men die just to say I tried to fight until the very end or make the call to get everyone in the bunker and give up. It's still secret and safe. The witches have shielded it from roaming eyes. Only wolves can see the entrance.'

My heart felt heavy at his words, and the fact that I wasn't there to help. Knowing that just giving myself up to the vampires could end the attack weighed heavily on me. *'The Ithaki broke a peace treaty and attacked here last night,'* I told him. *'They may attack while I'm gone...'*

Even though I wasn't alpha of the Paladins yet, I already felt an enormous responsibility to keep them safe.

'Tell them they can come to the bunker if things get bad there. I can have some of the witches get them in unnoticed,' Sawyer said.

That was a very kind offer, one I was going to tell Rab about.

'I'll tell them. And...Sawyer?'

'Yes, my wife?'

My throat constricted then. *'This is the shittiest honeymoon I've ever had.'*

He chuckled throatily, and the sound reverberated in my head, making my anxiety ease for a short time. *'I love your sense of humor as much as your pouty lips.'*

I smiled. *'But seriously, I want to tell you something. It's not giving up if you choose to save your men. Buildings can be rebuilt; lives can't be brought back from the dead.'*

I felt those words strike true inside of him.

'I know. I just... My first week as alpha and I've let everyone down. Our entire city will be a wasteland by the time this is over.'

I felt his failure, his disappointment, through the bond. He wanted to be a stronger alpha for his people, but he was given a shitty situation and he'd done the best he could with that.

'If it's a wasteland, we will rebuild with the Paladins, together, stronger than before, and we will have the defector witches too. We will be a safe haven for magical creatures who have nowhere to go.'

'You have big ideas, love. I'm just not that optimistic right now as I hide in a carved-out dirt hole in the ground and magic bombs go off around me.'

Sadness seeped into my soul. I could feel him dancing with depression. *'Then I'll be optimistic for the both of us. Get our people into the bunker, and I'll meet you there in three days' time, okay?'*

We'd reached the church now and the drums beat wildly, pulling my attention from Sawyer. Hundreds of Paladins were out on the lawn, and pride swelled in my chest when I saw that they were dressed in their finest clothes. They'd dressed up for me.

'Just give up?' Sawyer sounded lost, defeated.

'No. *Live to fight another day,'* I told him.

He sighed. *'You're right...we can't win this. We need to regroup. I'll make the call to get everyone down to the bunker and then instruct Eugene to bring you back to me in three days' time.'*

I smiled. *'Honeymoon in a bunker sounds kind of romantic.'*

I could feel his desperate urge to keep me safe, so strong it was suffocating. *'Come back to me, Demi.'*

'I promise,' I assured him, and then let Rab direct me over to the group of people who believed I would be strong enough to keep their magic alive.

As we stepped over to them, I let go of Sawyer and Wolf City and everything we'd just talked about. I trusted that Sawyer could take care of them, because I had my own issues with the Paladins to work out.

The hundreds of Paladin people were bent forward, banging wildly on their drums settled between their legs. The women had their hair braided neatly, with golden thread tying off the ends. They wore bright orange and red silks and vibrant blues. Small bone ornaments of different animals adorned their wrists. Sage stood behind the crowd, looking on at them in interest as Walsh and Eugene stood even farther back, watching it all with curious expressions. When I finally reached the crowd, the drums boomed one final time before stopping completely.

Small timid Astra looked like a confident queen as she strode over to me. Her hair was slicked back into a small ponytail at the nape of her neck. It was tied off with a strip of suede, and at the end hung stained bone beads in black and blue and gold. She'd rubbed some beetroot into her cheeks and on her lips, because they were stained a vibrant and pretty red. She looked beautiful. Wearing a long blue silk sari type of wrap dress, she bowed to me deeply. "Alpha."

I grinned, knowing now that she wasn't supposed to call me that until I'd proved myself. That every time she did, it was in direct defiance to Rab and the haters, showing support for me.

"Priestess." I bowed back.

When she stood, she straightened and faced the crowd around us. "Today, Demi will begin the alpha trial," Astra shouted. "Daughter of Running Spirit, granddaughter of Red Moon, she will leave her city ways behind and embrace nature, battle the beast of the Dark Woods, and claim the magic at the sacred cave in order to restore our people and our land!" Cheers of agreement rang out within the crowd.

Wait, battle the beast of the Dark Woods? Nobody said anything about that...

"From now on, she will be known to us as Spirit Moon." Astra bowed deeply again and my throat pinched with emotion. Running Spirit and Red Moon. She'd given me a name that was a combination of the two men who I never got to know but had a big part in why I was alive and here.

"Spirit Moon!" the crowd yelled, "Spirit Moon!"

Astra clapped her hands together and blue sparkly mist burst from her palms. The crowd fell into a hushed silence. The priestess crossed the lawn quickly and held her hands out, placing them on the top of my head.

"May the Father bless you and guide you, and may you return home to us quickly. I pray that your body is strong enough to be a vessel for our people's magic and that you will only get stronger with each day that you are away."

Leaning forward, she kissed my forehead and I had to swallow down my emotions.

I might not be religious or whatever, but she had clearly put a lot of effort into that prayer, which was super sweet, and I was grateful.

"Thank you, Astra."

Reaching behind her back, she brandished a small dagger. The handle was made of curved bone, and light glinted off the blade's razor-sharp steel edge. "This was

Red Moon's. He would want you to have it, and you can take one family heirloom into the trial."

My gaze glanced to Rab and he nodded. With that, I took the blade, grateful to have it, and stuck it into the belt at my waist.

Willow was among the drumming women, pregnant belly hanging over the rim of the drum. When I met her gaze, she gave me a nod.

"I won't let you down!" I yelled loudly for all to hear me. "I'll be back in three days with enough magic to light this place up like Christmas."

One by one, they put a fist over their chests in a sign of respect, and then Astra, Rab, and Sage led me away.

It was time.

We walked in companionable silence for a good thirty minutes, the whole time the drumming behind us getting softer and softer in the distance. The woods became thicker and darker, and a stench bled into the air as we neared what I assumed was the Dark Woods. The trees were gnarled, drier, and creepier here than in the Paladin village. It was also colder. I was going to freeze here at night!

Rab came to an abrupt stop, facing me. "This is as far as we can go." He pointed to a flat stone that was inset into the dirt: *Dark Woods. Alphas only. Enter at your own risk.*

Great.

I could still hear the drumming faintly.

101

"Someone will play the drum every hour on the hour for five minutes every day that you are gone to help you find your way home," Astra told me.

Wow, that was...a commitment. I nodded to her in thanks as Sage stepped forward.

"And I'll wait a week before I come in after your ass," Sage announced.

Rab's eyes widened. "*Don't* do that. These woods are cursed. Only a Paladin alpha can survive them. You wouldn't last a day."

Sage crossed her arms, glaring him down. "Cursed how? Some trees are going to know that I've stepped foot inside and kill me?"

Astra shared a nervous look with Rab, her eyes tracing the scar along his cheek.

"I was dared to go into the Dark Woods when I was younger." Rab swallowed hard and then reached up with one finger, tracing the line of his scar. "Let's just say the trees didn't appreciate that. They attacked me."

Sage stifled a laugh. "A *tree* attacked you? Sounds like you fell."

Rab shook his head, casting an irritated glance at her. "It moved, whacked me across the face the second I entered. Right over there." He pointed to a pile of rocks just behind the warning sign.

"Okay, no need for this talk," I assured everyone as Sage stared at the stack of rocks with a frown. "I'm coming right back."

"Of course you are," Sage agreed, and I loved her for her positivity in that moment.

I cleared my throat. "But first, Rab, I wanted to talk to you about something…"

He gave me a side-glance. "What is it?"

I could feel Sage and Astra's attention shift to us. There was no way of hiding this conversation, so I decided to just come out with it: "It looks like Sawyer is going to have to surrender in order to save everyone. He's going to take the rest of the city wolves into a large underground bunker that's hidden from all eyes that aren't wolf."

Rab frowned. "That's a hard call, but a strong one to make."

I nodded and faced him. "You should take everyone there and get them in the bunker too. Join the city wolves and regroup. Then when I get down there, we can all come up with a—"

"Join the city wolves? Leave our land?" he scoffed. "Is this the kind of alpha you will be? One that runs underground at the first sign of trouble?"

I narrowed my eyes at him. "First sign of trouble! You saw what happened last night. We nearly got a bomb dropped on us. Then the Ithaki attacked us. If it gets like that here, you need to get our people into the bunker!"

He sighed, and something dark crossed his face. "I'll leave it as a last resort. I sent three thousand more men to help Sawyer this morning. Surely we can win the war with that."

Three thousand more? That was great, and a lot, but I just didn't know if it was enough. "Maybe."

Rab placed two hands on my shoulders. "It will be my honor to call you alpha when you return. Just remember...giving up isn't an option." He squeezed my shoulders and I smiled.

That was all I was going to get out of him.

Astra hugged me as Rab stepped aside. "I'll pray for you every day."

I wrapped my arms around her, holding her tightly as love and respect filtered through our bond. When she pulled back, we both wiped our eyes, and then Sage was standing before me. I'd thought about this moment, this goodbye, all morning. Reaching onto my left hand, I pulled off my wedding ring and slipped it onto Sage's ring finger. "Keep it safe for me?"

Her lips pursed into a thin line as tears ran down her cheeks, and she nodded quickly.

"Hurry back, bitch. I love you." Sage pulled me in for a tight hug and we both broke into small sobs.

When we pulled away, I wiped her eyes and she wiped mine. "Sage...if I'm not back—"

"No," she growled.

I sighed. "Just take care of Sawyer, okay?"

She nodded, and I knew that I couldn't delay this any longer. Backing slowly into the Dark Woods, I raised my hand and waved to them.

"I'll be back in three days!" I shouted to everyone.

Rab just gave me a look that said, *Yeah, right,* but Astra and Sage nodded, waving me off.

I got this. Anyone could endure three days of hell. *Right?*

CHAPTER SEVEN

Three months later...

TODAY MARKED THREE MONTHS OF BEING IN THESE godforsaken woods, trying to find that damn magical cave. I had underestimated this task. Rab was right; these woods were cursed, haunted, *alive*. Every night while I slept, the trees rearranged themselves so that I couldn't memorize any path or visual markers to get out of here. I missed Sawyer so fucking much—Sage, Raven, my parents, the Paladins, people in general. Was the war over? Did we lose? Was Sawyer dead? My mind went wild all day long. The second I'd walked into the woods, I'd lost my ability to talk to him or even sense anything through our bond. I was completely cut off, but that was the least of my worries.

I looked down at my slightly bulging belly and whimpered.

My period was late. It was *so* fucking late that I

was pretty sure I was about three and a half months pregnant. I think I'd pinned it down to when we'd made love after Sawyer proposed. We'd had sex on the kitchen counter, on the bed, and then in the shower. The condom probably broke in the shower. Neither of us would have noticed. It didn't matter now; what mattered was that I was three months freaking preggo and lost in some magical ghost woods that hated me.

Alone.

Being pregnant, alone, and lost in creepy killer woods was not ideal, but by some saving grace I'd stumbled upon a bushcraft cabin on my fourth night here. It was full of handmade tools, clay pots, a small cot, and a fireplace. There were letters too, tons of little notes written on hand-pressed papyrus and scrolled with a burnt charcoal stick.

Run, Red Moon, Buffalo, and many before them had all added to this special place in the hopes that the next alpha would find it during their trial and have a place to stay while looking for the cave.

The notes kept me sane, made me feel like I wasn't alone, like I was just on a vacation reading a diary. I ran my fingers over the black chalk and read the note in my hands for the fiftieth time.

To my future kin,

The woods seem to change at night; don't go

looking for the cave without a sure way to trace your way back to the cabin.

We are one with this land, don't forget that. When you feel frustration, so do the woods.

—Red Moon

Then he had scratched something later. A hastily written note.

Does the cave hide from us? Only show itself when we are worthy?

I wanted to go back. I wanted to see Astra and find the beating of the drums and forget this whole thing. And I'd tried, twice. Once, on the twenty-sixth night, and once just last week. Both times I got lost and almost couldn't find my way back to the cabin. I wasn't proud of wanting to give up, but clearly this wasn't working. What I was doing *wasn't* working.

But even so, I had to keep trying or I'd lose my mind.

"Okay, baby girl. Ready for a little hike?" I patted my belly and then went to the far wall of the bushcraft cabin. It was still slightly exposed to the elements, made with intertwined branches and a thatch roof. I'd worked on covering it with mud, and after four attempts I'd found the right consistency to make a thick paste that was dry enough to be strong, yet wet enough to have good coverage.

"Leave the cabin better than you found it. Improve it for the future generations," I told no one, remembering the line Buffalo Moon, my great-great-great-grandfather had written on one of the papyruses. Grabbing my roll of twine, I started the task of tying it to my right ankle.

I'd chucked my underwear on day five. Now I wore a skirt made of an extra animal skin I'd found, and a top made of the same. They had puncture holes and ties so I could expand them as my belly grew, but I didn't plan on staying here much longer.

Today was the day I was finding the cave and getting out of here. I walked over to the place I'd mud pasted the most important note I'd found. From Run, my biological father.

Once you find the cave, the woods open and lead you home. Good luck.—Run

I stroked the cursive writing and smiled. *Thanks, Run.* This one single note kept me from losing my mind. It gave me hope, and hope was a powerful thing.

Walking outside, I tied off the end of the large ball of twine to one of the sticks I'd planted in the ground like a post. This was my true north, my safety net, my way home. I double-checked my water canteen was full and stashed some of the smoked rabbit meat I'd made this morning in my carrying pouch. Tapping my knife, which was tied to my inner thigh, and then the poison darts which I'd stashed in a satchel at my lower back, I nodded to the wind.

"Ready."

Heaving the endless loops of twine over my shoulder, I set out to find the magical cave. The morning sun had just risen, and I would do my customary four to six hours of cave hunting before catching dinner and heading to the cabin well before dark.

As I walked through the thick trees, I unwound the twine from my shoulder and let it fall behind me. I started out by singing Adele, then as I made my way up the mountain I shifted to Taylor Swift, and finally ended with the Jonas Brothers. Something about singing radio songs from my life at Delphi in Spokane made me feel normal. It also hid the weird sounds that came from deep within the forest, sounds that scared the crap out of me. Soft whistles, creaking wood, wet, slimy thwacks.

I shivered thinking of it. Nights were the worst. I tried to get all my sleeping in from about 4 p.m. to midnight. Or what I thought was 4 p.m. to midnight based on sunrise and sunset. Then I would stay awake listening to the trees rearranging themselves while I clutched my knife and tried to stay sane.

"Today is the day, baby girl. You're going to meet Daddy soon," I told her, the incline of the mountain getting steeper as I hiked.

If Daddy is still alive, I thought, and then scolded myself. I couldn't think like that. I needed to focus on getting out of here, restoring the magic to the Paladin people, and then finding Sawyer and my family.

Sweat dripped from my forehead as the morning sun rose high in the sky. The no-underwear thing was kind of cool because once you got a good breeze going up there, it was refreshing. Add that to things I never thought I would think.

Pulling out a hunk of the smoked rabbit meat, I chewed it and then chugged it down with water. I was worried I wasn't getting my folic acid or whatever was in those giant prenatal vitamins but I hadn't lost any weight thanks to finding the cabin and notes and all the tools. I had plenty of fish, rabbit, wild dandelion salad, small potatoes like tubers, and blueberries.

Take that, you paleo bitches.

I just hoped that was enough for my kid to be healthy. There were no pesticides or GMOs out here in the wild, so that was a step in the right direction, right?

Run had drawn a map to an artesian spring, where I hauled all of my water once a week. There was a creek where I caught the fish behind the cabin, but I thought I remembered reading that artesian water had vitamins and minerals in it, so I made the extra trip to haul that and drink it. I just told myself it was a folic acid artesian well and then stopped thinking about it. Nobody ever did their unborn baby good by worrying about things they couldn't change.

In a few more long strides, I reached the top of the mountain, the place that Run, Red, and every other alpha before me said the cave was, and my rope pulled taut as usual. The mountain didn't change, only the forest floor. I was okay to unhook and explore the mountain so long as I could make it back to this point. Untying the twine from my leg, I hooked it onto the peg stick I kept at the top of the path, then I sat down for a water break and planned out today's strategy.

To cover more ground, I'd call out my wolf and we'd both go hunting for it separately, something I'd been doing from the beginning to save time. The downside to that was that I found that too long with her outside of my body made me feel weak and exhausted. I think she was helping my body feed the baby or something, because once she rejoined me, I felt better. I didn't want to affect the baby's development, so I only pulled my wolf out for cave hunting or emergencies.

Shoving three more large strips of smoked rabbit into my mouth, I chewed quickly. I had no salt, no garlic, no pepper. It was just plain old gamey rabbit, but when it was all you had, it might as well be a gourmet burger with all the trimmings.

Calling my wolf forward, I watched as she crawled out of me in her semitransparent form and then looked up at me, tail wagging, when she was solid.

"Love you." I scratched her ears, knowing full well that telling her I loved her meant I was telling a part of myself I loved myself. I'd come to rely on these moments when she was outside of me, like having a loyal dog. It made me feel less alone.

"Go left, I'll go right, focus on smell. We haven't done that in a while," I told her.

'You got it,' she responded, and took off toward the well-worn path that led to the left, nose to the ground.

I took off to the right, stopping to scan the horizon, frowning at the dark mist that covered everything. Trees and mist as far as the eye could see, keeping me from seeing the Paladin lands or anything else.

Stupid haunted Dark Woods.

Inhaling through my nose, I took the path, skimming my fingers along the mountain wall to the left of me. I pressed in as I passed, looking for indents, or hidden handles, or anything suspicious. This path wound around the mountain all the way to the very top, where a single tree trunk stood with its branches shorn completely off. On the trunk were a bunch of names carved in deeply with a knife.

Red. Run. Midnight. Buffalo. East. Wind. I remembered them all by heart. I'd started adding my name and then stopped. I decided I would add it the day I found the cave instead. Leaning into the mountain wall, I inhaled. I was smelling for magic, those hot wires that I always smelled when I was near it. If the cave was full of magic, then surely it would smell of it, no?

"Your dad is going to be so excited when I tell him I'm pregnant." I spoke to my baby a lot. I had to or I feared I would lose my mind. I didn't know it was a "her," of course, but calling my baby "it" felt weird. "Like he

113

seriously will run out and buy fifty onesies the second I break the news." I grinned and rubbed my belly, which popped out slightly over the suede skirt I wore. "And obviously we'll have to get you some custom T-shirts to match mine." I pressed my fingers into the mountain, sniffing and even getting low in some parts in case it was a crawl-in entrance.

"*If poopy, get Daddy.*" I chuckled. "Ohh *Werewolf in training.* No. *Alpha in training*!" I told her, and then stopped as the hairs on my arms stood.

Nothing had happened, I mean not really, but... something felt different here. I spun around, sniffing the air and looking all over, trying to identify what had caused me to perk up. Was it...colder in this spot? I hadn't noticed before because it was winter, but... maybe it was the coolish breeze that had made me stop and given me chills. Leaning forward, I dug my fingers into the mountain, pulling away at ferns and soil, doing so wildly as I had many times before when I had a hunch I'd found something. Rocks and clumps of dirt rained down on my legs as I ripped at the ground, feeling my sanity crawling on a knife's edge.

"Come on!" I screamed, desperate to find the cave and leave this place, to go back to Sawyer and tell him I was carrying his child. My desperation was so strong I couldn't help the sob that left my throat. "Please! Help me!" I yelled at the mountain.

The creaking below got louder and I froze, turning

and looking down. There, in the thinnest parts of the mist, the trees...moved. Like possessed chess pieces, they ripped across the ground slowly, churning up soil. I closed my eyes, facing the mountain once more. I couldn't look at them moving. It unhinged me with fear.

We are one with this land, don't forget that. When you feel frustration, so do the woods, one of the letters had said. I had memorized them all.

I inhaled deeply through my nose and then exhaled slowly.

I sang a song my mother used to sing when I was a child to get me to sleep or calm me down: "Hush a bye, don't you cry, goooo to sleep, little baaaaby."

The trees stopped rustling and I opened my eyes, looking at the hole I'd dug in the side of the mountain. My fingernails were packed with dirt and there was no cave entrance.

Nothing.

I'd had some dark thoughts in my three months here all alone. But none so dark as the one I was having now: *What if I just stopped looking for the cave, if I just lived in that little hut and raised my baby in the woods, alone forever?*

The act of searching for the cave each day and not finding it, of trying to search for a way back to the Paladin lands and not finding it, *that* was what caused me so much stress. But what if I decided to stay? What if I let go of the idea of being *stuck* here and just made it home?

I whimpered.

No.

Too many people were counting on me. I shook myself, smacking my face lightly to snap myself out of it.

"Come on, Demi, pull it together. Be strong."

Ironically, thinking of Rab yelling at me and being disappointed in me spurred me on.

Shaking off those feelings, I trudged forward, working my feet into the well-worn footpaths, walking the same trail I walked every day. Some days I scaled up the side, but I had to stop once I realized I was pregnant.

One bad fall and...

Besides, one of the notes from Buffalo said, *I found it! It's right off the well-worn path. Plain as day once you trust.*

"Plain as day once you *trust*." What in the fuck did that mean? I didn't know but I thought about it every night before I went to bed. It looped around my mind until I drifted off.

Plain as day once you trust.

Trust what! My wolf? The land? The Paladins? God? I mean, I'd racked my damn mind for days on that.

'*Find anything?*' I checked in with my wolf and pressed on, winding higher and higher up the mountain until I reached the wooden tree stub at the top.

'*Nothing.*'

I collapsed at the base of the tree trunk, pulling the canteen to my lips, and took a long swig. My heart raced and my legs ached, and admittedly I was feeling extra depressed today. Hunger pangs tightened my gut and I shoved the last two hunks of rabbit meat into my mouth and swallowed them. Not a moment later, I heard the padding of my wolf's paws.

'You're going to need to start taking it easy. I think you're burning too many calories.' My wolf looked at me from her place perched before me. I was hungry all the time. My belly was definitely growing, because I'd had to poke another hole in the waistband of the skirt, but my arms did look a bit thinner...my thighs too.

My wolf is right.

"I'll cave hunt every other day starting next month," I told her, and then winced at the fact that I was making plans to be here for another freaking month!

I was so tired, I just lay there for a good thirty minutes watching the clouds go past. I dozed off a few times, but my wolf licked me awake by midafternoon. She knew we couldn't be caught up here after dark, and I still had to catch tonight's dinner and tomorrow's breakfast.

"Okay. Time to head back down. I'll take the trail you took and you take the trail I took," I told her.

It was what we always did, to be sure that we both covered each area twice. She cocked her head to the side. *'You seem more tired than normal. I'm going to join you. One day without double-checking both sides of the mountain won't hurt—'*

"Yes it will!" I snapped and then frowned. "I'm sorry,

but we *have* to check both sides like we always do. What if you missed something, or what if I did? We have to."

I'd had a wild thought recently. What if the cave only opened one day a year? What if on that day Run had decided to go another path and that's why it took him three years?

I was going to check both sides of this mountain every single day so long as I was able.

She walked over and nuzzled my belly. '*Okay. But soon we stop pushing so hard.*'

"Soon, I promise," I told her.

As I stood, we split off, and I gathered a few tubers and mushrooms on my way down, as well as a quail I found in one of my traps. It would make an amazing soup. When my wolf and I both reached the twine tied to the stick, I put it around my ankle and she joined my body, giving me an immediate boost of energy.

'*Thanks, girl,*' I told her, and headed back to the cabin, winding the twine around my shoulder and elbow as I went.

I hummed a little tune all the way back to the house, where I set into my normal dinner routine. Filling the clay pot with artesian spring water, I suspended it over the fire to heat the water for my soup, and then set about making the mud mixture for the outside of the cabin to keep me busy while I waited.

Leave it better than you found it. This would keep bugs out and insulate it from the cold winter winds. It also gave me something to do, which I think was part of why all of the alphas before me did the same.

There was a main cabin with a single open space about twelve feet by twelve feet, and then a bathhouse, which was essentially a tiny four-foot-square hut with a thatched roof. Suspended from the roof was a clay pot with holes in the bottom that trickled the water I poured inside when I took my nightly shower.

I couldn't think up a better system, so I left that as is since it did the job. Anytime I needed to go to the bathroom, I just went in the woods. It was a simple life, but it worked.

Once my stew was done, I gulped it down greedily, moaning at the flavor the mushrooms and tubers had given the quail. Defeathering a bird and ripping out its guts had horrified me my first week out here, but then I just became so hungry I no longer cared. Now I did it on autopilot, completely desensitized to the whole thing. Same with fish. I didn't go for big game like deer and such yet because I wasn't sure what to do with all that meat and this was working just fine for one person. I could smoke it, but that would only last for a day or so. I could try my hand at dehydrating, but you needed low heat for that, and I wasn't sure I could control the fire that well.

A problem for another day.

Before I knew it, I'd eaten the entire large clay pot of stew...

So much for breakfast tomorrow. I'd have to hunt in the morning, or at the very least gather some berries.

After rinsing the pot in the clay sink with some of my stored water, I set it outside the window and let it dry on the sill. There was still plenty of light out and I was exhausted. Better get some rest before the night shift of listening to creepy noises as the forest moved around me. I drank some water and peeled off my suede skirt and top, slipping into the cot naked. The sleeping pad that sat atop the cot was mercifully packed with thick cotton buds and not too bad comfort-wise. I slipped my hunting blade under the suede pillow packed with cotton, and then pulled another suede blanket over me. Everything here was made of some type of animal skin, but I was thinking with all of this cotton growing out in the wild that I might be able to make a loom with some of the twine...

I rolled on my side and stroked my belly, trying not to think of raising a child in this small hut. Should I start weaving a bassinet? Or did that mean I was giving up? *Maybe I should give up. Maybe I should just go tomorrow and search for the Paladin lands until I run out of food and water.* I shook my head to try and shake off the dark thoughts.

No. I could do this. Find the cave, go home, and get back to Sawyer.

My eyelids grew heavy and then...

Boom.

A kick bucked against my hand and I gasped.

She kicked.

She kicked!

"Is that you, baby girl?" It felt like a troop of butterflies had taken flight in my belly and then knocked. Another one!

It was such a joyous moment that quickly turned to dread as I had no one to share it with.

'Sawyer,' I reached out for the millionth time. *'Sawyer, we have a baby girl and she just kicked for the first time,'* I told him.

His silence was the most depressing part of each day. I was afraid that one day the loneliness might actually consume me.

With a deep sigh, I thought about the line Buffalo had written.

I found it! It's right off the well-worn path. Plain as day once you trust.

Trust who? I just wished he'd told me who I needed to trust.

Trust.

Trust?

I drifted off with little hope that I would make it out of here. I just had to trust.

CHAPTER EIGHT

Three months later...

WALKING IN THE WOODS, GOING TO FIND THE caaaaave," I sang as I waddled through the bushes and up the mountain. I was so preggo, I couldn't see my feet anymore. My hips and back hurt and I was down to weekly cave searches. It was too exhausting, and I was starting to have contractions on cave-hunt day, which I knew it was too early for, so I had to take it easy. Walk slow: one trip up the mountain with my wolf inside of me and hope for the best. I'd become completely numb to the fact that I'd been here six months. I'd tried one more time to find the Paladin lands last month and got lost coming back. It took me five days to find the cabin.

Five days alone in the woods with no shelter and no sure source of running water was terrifying, especially when pregnant, but I'd learned so much in my time here that I was able to find food and water pretty easily. Now

I'd resigned myself to the fact that the woods would not let me leave until I had found the cave. So I had two options. Find the cave or stay here and live out my days in nature forever.

I sighed, trying not to fall into a depressive episode. Last week I'd just lain around the cabin, only getting up to hunt or wash, and I recognized symptoms of what was probably depression.

How the hell was I going to raise a baby here, alone, possibly forever? I was a social creature; I needed human interaction and Instagram and people to talk to. The baby would help. I could talk to her, but…Sawyer, my parents…what were they thinking and doing right now? Were Sage and Astra losing their minds? I'd have bet Rab was like, *I told you she would take forever.*

"ARGH!" I yelled at the mountain as I reached the top and bent to untie my ankle string.

A female moan ripped through the woods, and I froze, fingers hovering over the knot on my ankle as goose bumps ran up my arms.

No. No. No.

The day had finally come. I was hallucinating, hearing voices. The noises from the woods were tricking me.

"Hello!" I shouted as I pulled my hunting knife from my thigh holster.

It wasn't real, probably just a tree moving, not—

A distinct feminine moan, similar to an injured animal, called back to me.

What the hell?

My heart leaped in my throat, and I looked up the mountain path where I was supposed to go, before glancing out into the darkness of the woods where the noise came from.

Was it a trap? Was it a person who needed help? How was that even possible?

You're not real. It's not real. I chewed my lip, feeling the nervous breakdown threatening to consume me.

There was another moan that gave way to a whimper and I froze. If someone *was* out there, I had to know for sure. Diverting from the beaten path that would lead me up the mountain, I went sideways and to the left, slowly. This led away from the cabin, away from the cave, but nearer the direction I thought the Paladin lands were.

Would someone have come looking for me? I didn't allow myself to hope such a thing, especially since Rab said whoever crossed over into the Dark Woods and was not of alpha bloodline would be cursed. But...maybe it was a fey or a troll or someone else. Anyone else would do. If they were hurt, I could nurse them back to health and then I'd have a friend here. I'd best-friend the shit out of a dark fey right now, I was that desperate and lonely.

Spurred on by these exciting thoughts, I slowly trudged through the thick forest bramble, coaxing the twine behind me so that it didn't get caught on anything and tear. My belly was large, but the baby was sitting pretty high, so I was able to move with ease across the mountainside without too much trouble. One thing being in the Dark Woods had done was get me in shape. You either got in the best shape of your life out here or you died. I didn't mean that I was skinny. I was strong, with endurance and mental aptitude I just didn't have before I came here.

"Hello?" I called again, wondering if I was leading myself into a trap. So far for six months, I hadn't seen another soul, but that didn't mean that people didn't travel through here. I'd seen bear, deer, fox, rabbit, elk, a whole host of animals, but no people.

"Hephgmn." Someone tried to speak, but it was muffled, and there was a sick gargling noise to it that made the hair rise on the back of my neck.

The female tone to the voice was the only thing that spurred me forward. It reminded me of Marmal and how she'd saved me from being near death.

What if I could do that for another?

"I'm coming!" I shouted, and ran faster, holding my belly with my right arm to keep it from jostling the baby too much, and gripping the twine with my left. I was running so fast, so focused on the sound of the woman, that I didn't realize the string was getting shorter until it pulled taut, yanking my ankle out from under me. With a hiss, I threw both hands out and caught my fall as I stumbled onto my knees.

That was close.

I needed to slow down or I could hurt the baby. The

twine was pinching my ankle and I knew that if I wanted to go after whoever this voice was, I needed to leave it and venture a bit farther...blind. The thought scared me, but I couldn't leave a woman out here to die and miss out on my chance at having a companion.

"I'm coming!" I shouted one more time as I untied the twine and ripped a nearby branch off, pinning the twine into the earth like you would stake a tent. The trees might move while I was gone and yank the twine away, so this was the best I could do.

I popped to my feet and got my bearings. "One more sound! Just one more and I've got you," I called out into the woods.

"Mmmmm!" they grunted deeply, and my hands shook as I spied a naked leg peeking out from beneath a tree trunk. Pulling my knife, I stalked slowly toward the leg, wondering where the hell the rest of the person was. Then I realized what I was seeing. The tree had fallen on her, and she was hanging down the hillside, where I couldn't see the rest of her body obscured by the large trunk.

"I see you!" I cried out, and then looked back over my shoulder to make sure I had a good sense of where I'd left the twine rope tied off. I could see it; I had a good sense of direction. Turning back around, I scrambled the last fifty feet with my heart in my throat.

The one exposed leg was wearing a familiar black Nike tennis shoe...and I really wondered if I'd lost my mind and was hallucinating. I didn't think so because everything about this encounter was terrifyingly real.

Peering over the top of the log, a sob ripped through my throat.

A shock of red hair splayed out in a fan. It was Sage lying face down in the dirt, the heavy tree pressed across her entire back, pinning her into the ground. I'd know that red hair anywhere, and I stood there for a moment in complete shock that she'd come looking for me.

"Sage!" I half sobbed. "I've got you. I'm getting this off of you," I screamed as she began to weep, her whole body shaking with sobs. I scrambled backward and looked for a large sturdy tree branch that I could use as leverage to roll the log off of her. I was over six months preggo and there was no way I was going to try to deadlift that thing and have my baby come early.

I'd made a lot of improvements to the cabin land over the last three months, building a small nursery addition to the main cabin, and I'd done so by using a lever and pulley system to move heavy logs.

There! I spotted the perfect fallen tree limb and grabbed it, quickly snapping away useless branches until just the large staff was left. Running back over to Sage, I tried to mentally work out whether I should roll the log down over her head using gravity but risk hurting her brain, or over her legs and risk breaking an ankle...

You could heal a broken ankle in the woods but not a broken brain. Positioning myself at her head, I wedged the staff under the log and she screamed in pain, until I realized I'd stabbed her arm, which was trapped beneath the log as well.

"Shit, I'm sorry." Moving a few inches over, I tried again and got a good firm grip on the staff. "I'm going to roll it off you...but it might hurt."

She didn't say anything, and I took that as a sign that she'd either passed out or consented. One. Two...

"Now!" I shouted, and jumped up into the air, bringing all of my weight down on the staff. The giant log popped free of her back and rolled over her butt, slamming down on the backside of her knees.

A wail of complete misery ripped through the forest and tears rolled down my face. I'd unpinned her arms, but she hadn't moved them, and I didn't know if that was because she was scared to or paralyzed.

"One more and that's it," I told her. "Hang on." Wedging the wood under the log again, I leaped into the air and came down with all of my weight. The giant log popped up and then rolled off of her tennis shoes, barely missing her ankles.

She was free.

Panting, I fell to my knees and brushed the red hair off her face before bursting into quiet sobs—I barely recognized my bestie.

She had three thin scars running from her eye to her chin, dirt and blood caked her eyebrows, and her once fierce look she always wore was now dull and hopeless.

I took in her dirty, torn clothing, and her handmade suede backpack. She'd been here awhile...maybe even months.

I was having a hard time believing this was real. Maybe I was imagining her because I'd been so lonely... but why would I imagine Sage hurt like this?

I wouldn't.

"You came for me." I cupped her cheek, getting onto my elbows so that she could see me at her odd angle. Her neck was bent weird and she hadn't moved and I didn't know what to do.

Her vacant eyes searched my face, and she chewed on her lip before looking past me at nothing. "Rab was right. I'm cursed. This whole place is cursed." Then her entire body shuddered and she went limp.

———·———

It took me nearly three hours to get Sage back to my cabin. I had to take off my large suede skirt, lay her on it, and then fashion a harness with the twine so that my wolf could drag her like a pack mule. Every time we went over a rocky area, Sage would roll off my skirt, and twice the holes in the suede just ripped and the twine flew out. I had to braid it to make it thicker, and it was digging into my wolf's shoulders, but she didn't complain.

Once we'd finally gotten her back, I threw on another

skirt, a short one that sat under my giant belly, and lay Sage in front of my cot on the floor. She was too heavy for me or my wolf to lift into my bed, and I wasn't sure moving her more than we had to was a good idea.

She looked...near death. Her body was covered in scars and bruises, ranging from blue to yellow, and I wondered if her werewolf healing could handle a broken back or internal bleeding or whatever might be going on.

I sat there, chewing off all of my fingernails, wondering just how long she'd been out here looking for me—surely she didn't come in a week after I left like she joked she would.

She was *joking*, right?

And what in the hell had she meant by being cursed? I stared at her, wondering what in the hell to do, when my survival mode finally kicked in.

I hadn't hunted today. I had no refrigerator, and other than some mushrooms, dried dandelions for tea, and a few sweet potatoes, I had *nothing* to eat. I couldn't help Sage right now. I wasn't a doctor and I didn't have an MRI, but I could hunt so that when she hopefully woke up, there would be a hot meal for the both of us.

Staring at the steady rise and fall of her chest, I decided to just focus on what I could control or I would lose my mind with worry. Grabbing my spear and net, I set out to the creek behind the cabin to catch some fresh fish.

Okay, Sage was here, near death, but I wasn't alone anymore. One of those two things was very cool. I needed to focus on the positive.

The baby kicked then, and I reached down and rubbed my belly. "It's okay. Mama's got this."

After about an hour of spearfishing, I'd caught six fish. I normally only caught about two or three before heading back, because I had no need for an excess of fish that would just rot on my wood block kitchen counter, but I was hunting for Sage now too, a thought that brought me untold happiness.

"I'm not alone," I mumbled to myself, unsure if the gravity of that sentence actually had sunken in yet. "I'm...not alone." I stopped at the edge of the creek, fish in my net, and broke into sobs.

I'm not alone anymore.

My best friend came into the cursed woods to look for me and nearly died. Did I even deserve that kind of friendship? I wasn't sure. I had to make sure Sage got through this. I had to take care of her.

I wiped my tears, gathering myself and then headed back to the cabin. The second I neared, I sensed something was wrong. One of my clay pots outside was tipped over, broken, and I could hear weird huffing animal sounds. When I rounded the corner, the sight of a giant black bear caused me to stop dead in my tracks.

"Go on!" I shouted. "Get!" I raised my arms to make myself look big.

The bear was peeking inside the open cabin door, right at Sage! I'd seen bears off and on around here but always from a distance. They never came into my camp and I never kept food overnight. If I did, I tied it up in the trees in a satchel. I knew enough about camping to do that.

What I wouldn't give for Marmal's shotgun right now.

"Hey, bear!" I shouted, and reached down to grab a rock, chucking it at his back. My wolf stirred, sensing the impending danger, and in the blink of an eye she was out of my body and had solidified by my side. The bear backed away from the door and turned to face me, his nostrils flaring as he no doubt smelled the fish in the net that I held.

I was *not* giving up my dinner! Sage needed this meat to get better.

Since I'd gotten here, there had been little use for my magic. Running vampire fast didn't help when searching for a hidden cave opening, you had to go slow for that, and there were no bullets to stop out here either. So I'd just gotten used to being a regular old werewolf, but now that I was faced with this threat, I felt my magic stirring. The scent of hot wires filled the air.

I set the net containing the fish down on the ground and then stepped closer to the bear.

"Get. *Out*," I growled.

My wolf dipped her head low; her lips peeled back to reveal her pointed teeth, then a deep, terrifying growl ripped from the back of her throat. The bear sniffed the air again and immediately jerked backward as if he'd smelled my magic and knew what it meant. Taking one last look inside of the cabin at Sage, he turned and ran away, heading toward the creek to hopefully catch his own damned fish.

I relaxed, my magic fizzling as weakness took hold of me. I couldn't handle my wolf being outside of my body for too long anymore, and already having her out for so many hours while she dragged Sage here, it was taking its toll.

As if sensing this, she leaped into my chest. I picked up the fish and headed back to the cabin. When I got inside, I was relieved to see Sage's wolf curled into a ball, her chest rising and falling in rapid pants. That was a good sign. If she was alive enough to shift, that meant she was going to make it.

Right?

She would heal faster in wolf form.

I went about the work of gutting and deboning the fish, tossing cubes of it into my clay cooking pot with wild mushrooms, sliced sweet potatoes, and some wild green onions that had just started to spring up around the creek.

Once the food was boiling on the rack above the fireplace, I set out to make another bedroll. I'd been collecting cotton so that I could try to make a bassinet for the baby, and maybe even a winter sleeping bag of sorts, but all of that would have to wait.

Sage was here.

The very thought had me looking down at her to make sure she was real.

Using a bone needle and twine, I pierced the edges of two large pieces of suede cloth and started to make a sleeping mat. I was sure it was going to be comfortable, but the stitch work needed help. I just didn't care. I was too tired and too excited and nervous for Sage to be here. Once I had roughly sewn three sides together, I started to shove the cotton inside. I'd already shelled it and picked off the little hard bits that were left over, including the seeds. Then I'd pulled the buds apart, making it fluffier and as big as possible. By the time I stitched the top of the mat, I'd gone through all the cotton I'd harvested for the baby, but I had made a four-inch-thick mat for Sage to sleep on.

I had one deer skin left, and I could probably harvest another before I went into labor. I'd started hunting big game recently, knowing that when the baby came, I would need things like animal skins to keep her warm in the winter. I took what meat I could and left the rest for other animals nearby.

Shaking off those thoughts, I stepped back inside the hut and lay the mat in front of Sage's wolf, who was still asleep. The scents of the delicious fish soup had completely saturated the cabin, and I was so starved I wasn't going to be able to wait for her to wake up.

Pulling the pot off the fire, I set it on the ground

and grabbed a clay bowl and matching spoon. I'd tried many times to replicate whoever had made these, but whenever I tried to fire them like you would in a kiln, they cracked. Whatever skill the person who had made these had, I wasn't going to learn it anytime soon. Pouring myself a large bowl, I scarfed it down while I watched Sage sleep.

"Sage," I called to her in between slurps.

Her wolf stirred slightly but stayed fast asleep, panting in a heavy rhythm.

"Hungry? Thirsty?" I sucked down the last bit of my soup and then poured a large bowl for her from the clay pot, using the same bowl and spoon. There was only one set, so we were going to have to share from now on.

From now on. I wanted to cry at the fact that I wasn't alone anymore. The steam from the soup filtered up to the roof of the cabin as I watched Sage's wolf and prayed she would wake up and be okay.

Running my fingers through my hair to detangle it, I pulled it into a tight braid and then brushed my teeth with some clay powder and ground mint leaves. Sometimes I had silly thoughts like the fact that I could probably sell this homemade toothpaste to the hippies back in Spokane for like nine bucks a small clay pot.

After rubbing my teeth vigorously with the dried abrasive moss brush I'd made, I spit into the sink.

"Holy *shit*, you're pregnant!" Sage screeched in a weak and raspy voice, and I jumped backward so quickly I nearly tripped over the bowl of soup I'd put down for her.

I looked down at my best friend, wide-eyed, heart pounding in my chest.

She spoke...that meant... "You're real?" Tears streamed down my face.

The scars on her cheek were still there, like she'd been attacked by an animal, and so was the bruising, but she was talking and breathing and sitting up...so that was good.

Reaching out, she pulled my suede blanket over her naked body and took in a few deep breaths. "Are you *really* pregnant? Or am I hallucinating?" she questioned again, her eyes on my belly.

I chewed my bottom lip, nodding as more tears fell, and then I dropped to my knees before her. "From the night Sawyer proposed, I think."

She burst into crying laughter and reached out to lay a hand on either side of my swollen tummy. As she extended her right arm, she winced and retracted it. With her left, she stroked my stomach, looking at it wide-eyed. "Demi...you're *fucking* pregnant."

Now it was my turn to burst into crying laughter as she pulled me into a hug, cradling her obviously injured arm between us.

"I'm so...glad you're here," I said, between sobbing and laughing like I'd lost my mind. "How long have you been here?"

I felt like being social was hard for me right now, like six months without a conversation with another human had made me a bit strange, and I needed to relearn eye contact and pausing to let others speak and all of those things you would teach a child.

When she pulled back, she looked at my belly and then at the soup. "Is that...?"

She seemed about as socially awkward as I was.

I nodded. "For you."

She looked skeptical. "I won't take food from a pregnant lady. Are you sure you've had enough?"

A grin pulled at the corners of my lips. "I have, and there's more." I pointed to the steaming pot in the corner at the hearth of the fireplace. Without another word, she grabbed the soup bowl and started to chug, only stopping when a chunk of fish or potato made it in her mouth, and even then she only chewed once or twice. She'd lost weight, her hair was caked in dirt and blood, and she smelled like a zoo.

"Sage, how long have you been here in the woods?"

She shook herself, moaning as the last bit of soup went down her throat. "Forever? I lost count. It got too depressing so I stopped." She looked behind me, to the doorway, as if expecting someone to charge in and attack her.

I frowned. "How long did you wait for me before you came after me?" I'd kept a meticulous daily count. If she told me how many months she'd waited until coming after me...

"A week. Like I said." She looked at me then with a fierce protectiveness and my whole body froze, my throat tightening with emotion.

"Sage...you've been here five months and three weeks. How did you survive?"

She chewed her lip and I could see that I had fared much better than she had. There were so many scars; she was too skinny, too unhinged, paranoid even. Why did she keep looking at the door?

Her bottom lip quivered. "Same as you. Drink from the creeks, hunt small game, forage. Sleep under the trees."

But that's *not* what I had been doing. I'd had a home, letters to read, a shower, a place to go to each night and have a sense of normalcy.

Her eyes flicked to the door once more, and I reached out and grasped her hand, causing her to jump.

"Sage? What did you mean about you being cursed?"

Her gaze flicked from the door to me again and she swallowed hard. "I shouldn't have come here. It will bring trouble to you. I need to go." She moved to stand, but I yanked her down with surprising force and she winced as if in pain, causing me to loosen my hold.

"Sorry, but, Sage, I've been alone for *six months*. I'm pregnant and stuck here. You are *not* leaving me no matter what trouble you may bring, and I'm not leaving you either."

She pulled her hand from mine then and burst into

tears, cupping her face as she rocked back and forth. "It will know I'm here," she wailed. "You might get hurt."

My heart broke in that moment for my poor friend, who was clearly on the edge of a mental breakdown. I'd been there, so many times I'd been there.

"Just calm down. We will figure this out together. What is *it*?" I rubbed her back softly as she sobbed.

She pulled her hands from her face, showcasing cheeks stained by tears, which had run through the brown dirt and crimson blood, leaving tracks on her face.

"The curse, the magic, the woods. It *hates* me. It's trying to *kill* me. Rab was right," she whispered as if *it* could hear her.

Maybe she'd eaten some bad mushrooms or something and was hallucinating. "Okay, well, if *it* comes, we can fight it together." I smiled, trying to brush the whole thing over.

She shook her head and then pointed to the three lined scars that ran down her cheek. "Last time I did that, this happened."

Something clicked in my mind then. "Wait, are you talking about the bear?"

She looked out the door, eyes wide. "The bear, the elk, the mountain lions, the *trees*. They're all trying to kill me for coming here. I'm not wanted here," she told me, and lifted her shirt to reveal a puckered scar.

My mouth popped open in shock as things started to click in my mind.

The moving trees, the bear sniffing inside my cabin... was he specifically hunting Sage? Was Rab right about the curse?

"What's that from?" I asked, pointing to the scar.

"Elk attack, while I was sleeping."

Elk attack? Elk didn't just randomly attack sleeping people. "The tree," I whispered.

She nodded. "Threw itself at me and knocked me into the ground. I would have died without your help."

Holy shit. Holy, holy fucking shit.

Okay...my best friend had been stuck in killer woods for over five months searching for me and now we had no way out. No big deal...I could handle this.

"Okay. Well...I'm an alpha and the woods don't hurt me and neither do the animals, so you're safe with me now."

I hoped saying it would make it true.

She looked at me with pity, like she wanted to believe that, but there was no way she could.

"So if you left a week after I did...is the war...?" *Please give me good news.* I just needed good news about the outside world.

Sage swallowed hard, looking down at my belly again like she maybe didn't want to tell me something that might upset me.

"Sage. Is Sawyer okay?"

She nodded. "He's fine, but we lost the war. Everyone, including nearly all of the Paladins, went underground and are safe in hiding as far as I know."

I sagged in relief. Sucked to learn we'd lost the war, but good to know our people were alive. I could deal with that. "So Sawyer is in the bunker?" That was good. It meant he was with my parents.

Sage chewed her lip.

"Sage!"

She sighed. "Sawyer commanded that Walsh get everyone into the bunker and stay there to look after your parents and his mom. Astra stayed in Paladin Village to beat that stupid drum every hour."

My throat closed with emotion at that. Sweet Astra. I hoped she was okay.

"And Sawyer?"

Sage frowned. "He and Eugene said they would wait to go into the bunker until you got back."

My eyes widened. "So he just stayed out in the open in the middle of a war!"

Sage winced. "He hid obviously, but I don't know how well... He could have been captured."

Captured! I burst to my feet and started to pace the small room, made even smaller with Sage and her mat on the floor.

"Or not... I don't really know. Maybe he went into the bunker..."

I stopped my pacing and settled. Yeah, maybe...

Except I knew Sawyer, and he wasn't the type to hide and wait to be saved.

Frick.

A long stretch of silence passed between us. I didn't know what to say, and clearly neither did she.

"Did you make this place?" She looked around at the cabin and I was grateful for the topic change.

I shook my head. "Past alphas did, but I improved on it. It's got a shower. Want one? I can start boiling the water." No sense in worrying about Sawyer and my family until I was out and able to do something about it.

Her eyes widened. "YES I want a shower, have you lost your mind? What kind of question is that? Do you have soap?"

I chuckled. "No, but I have an exfoliating clay scrub with lavender."

She grinned. "That sounds like heaven."

I boiled the water and then helped her stand. She had a limp on her right side, the leg that had been bent at an odd angle when I'd found her. With a little help, I was able to get her into the shower and fill the clay pot overhead with warm water.

"Ohmygod, this is heaven!" she screamed as I stood outside the small shower hut and peered into the woods with paranoia. Would that bear come back? Would an elk? What she'd said was so weird, I wasn't sure how to process it.

Were the Dark Woods trying to kill Sage? If so, she

might be safer here in the pasture with the cabin. It was free of large trees, and if we could erect some kind of fence, it might deter the animals...

"Are you seriously here?" Sage called through the thatched siding.

I grinned. It was weird how easily we were falling back into our normal banter.

"I know; I can't believe it," I told her.

"So, I can start helping you look for the cave now and we can be out of here in a few weeks I'll bet!" she said excitedly.

Oh. She still had that optimism I'd had three months ago.

"Yeah, maybe," I said.

Now that Sage was here, I was less interested in searching for the cave and more so in preparing to safely have this baby.

CHAPTER NINE

Three months later...

S TOP GETTING UP," SAGE BARKED AS SHE FUSSED OVER me. "Just lie around like the giant pregnant lady you are and let me do stuff!"

I chuckled. My belly was the size of the moon and my ankles were slightly swollen.

Sage pulled my feet up to prop them onto the bassinet we'd woven to prepare for the baby, and then she went back to skinning the rabbit she'd caught for dinner. She was such a huge help these past three months, I'm not sure I would have made it without her.

"I'm pregnant, not useless," I told her with a grin. That was partially a lie, I was so pregnant I was basically useless, but I felt stir-crazy. Sage had forced me into bed rest two weeks ago when my ankles got swollen so bad that we could see my thumb indent when I pressed on them.

Sage pointed her deadly hunting blade at me and narrowed her eyes. "Don't mess with me, woman. I have a knife."

My grin grew wider. Sage and I had made a pact last night. We were going to give up looking for the cave for the next three months. It was so disheartening to climb all the way up there week after week and have the same results. We were defeated and *so fucking over it.*

It was time to just prepare for this baby. It was time to look forward to something. We also made a pact to stop talking about the past as well. It was too painful. It had been nine months. Sawyer was either dead, captured, or underground. Willow had given birth already and her baby would be human. The Ithaki probably invaded Paladin Village and killed Astra...

I'd failed them all.

It was better for my mental health if I just didn't think about it, so I shoved it into a deep dark box in my psyche and didn't go there.

The bear and elk and other possessed animals only seemed to attempt attacking Sage when I wasn't around, so we went everywhere together, which was fine by me. The curse was real. I'd seen enough over the past three months to believe that.

Sage held up the perfect fluffy white rabbit skin pelt and grinned. "I think we have enough for the winter baby blanket."

I nodded. "Definitely. We can stitch it up today."

We'd prepared for the birth as best we could for two women who knew jack shit about having babies. The biggest issue was the placenta. I knew you had to clamp the cord before you cut it or you'd risk losing all of the baby's blood. We gathered all the knowledge we had about labor from every movie I'd seen, or stories she'd heard of, and we decided that the scene from *Wanderlust* where the hippie chick carries the placenta around in a bowl next to her baby until it naturally falls off was safest.

I was young and healthy. We had no reason to believe giving birth would have any serious complications. "Back in the Renaissance times, fourteen-year-olds popped out a baby a year and had no idea what they were doing," Sage had told me.

I had no idea if it was true, but it made me feel better.

The swollen feet were likely because I did a lot of hiking and housework, more than a normal pregnant lady who lived in the city. Even with Sage's help, there was so much work to do.

But everything was going to be fine. I truly felt that in my bones.

"Your boobs are getting gigantic. Sawyer would be sad to miss this," Sage said, and then her face fell when she realized she'd spoken of the past. "Sorry."

I gave her a light smile, trying to pretend I wasn't fazed by the comment. "Yeah."

Sage and I had endless conversations about what the note I'd plastered to the wall meant.

I found it! It's right off the well-worn path. Plain as day once you trust.

We'd decided that he meant to finish it, trust...and never did, or it had been erased. No one would be that cruel, right?

"Trust *what*?" I would scream on a daily basis. But not today. Today, we had decided to not talk about or go looking for the cave. Today, we were a mom-to-be and auntie-to-be, excited about a baby.

For the next three months, I was just going to focus on being a mom with my best friend, and worry about everything else after that.

"If you want to name her after me, I won't care. I mean, I am going to be the best aunt ever." Sage plopped the rabbit meat into the pot.

I chuckled. "Yeah, that won't be confusing at all, calling both of you Sag—" I gasped, clutching my belly as it tightened and went rock-hard.

Sage froze. "Braxton Hicks?"

The pain was intense, so intense that I couldn't speak for a moment.

"Maybe?" I said, breaking out in a sweat. I'd been getting a lot of these false-labor belly-tightening things over the past month, but that one was...different.

She stood, rushing around the cabin and into the adjoining nursery room I'd created. "We are going to pretend labor has started anyway, okay? I don't want your water breaking on the mattress pad."

She was right. We'd talked about the birthing plan, and we both agreed we should try to keep the beds from irreversible damage, as there was no replacing them.

"Okay, but I think it's another false alarm." I'd had a lot of those this week.

Moving to stand and make my way into the adjoining room that Sage had prepared as a birthing room, I was racked with another painful contraction midstride.

Okay...this was more than the fake contractions I'd been having all week. I rush-waddled into the room to find Sage laying out the deerskin suede on top of the clay bricks I'd fired. I'd finally mastered the art of firing clay in a deep hole inside the earth. I just dug a hole, put the pots or bricks inside that I had shaped from the natural clay mud, and then shoved a bunch of twigs and dried grasses in there and lit them.

It worked! This was a game changer. Sage even made the baby a little clay rattle with stones inside; it was adorable.

"I think it might be the real thing," I told her just as wetness trickled down my legs. I froze, looking down at the clear fluid dripping to the floor.

Looking up, I met Sage's panicked gaze. "Okay, it's go time! I'm gonna boil water and wash my hands."

Holy crap.

Okay...it was time. After all these months of preparing, I was about to have a baby out in the woods with no pain meds.

"Remember all those movies you told me about that had the women on their hands and knees?" Sage asked.

I nodded, slipping free of my giant loose dress and sitting naked and cross-legged on the floor. Sage and I had seen each other naked a hundred times; this was going to be no big deal.

"I think you should try that, on all fours, and then sitting or rocking might help the baby come out?"

Being on my back with all this belly weight pressing down on me was hard anyway, so that was a good idea.

"Maybe I should shower," I called out into the house as Sage had disappeared. "What if there is bacteria on my legs and it gets on the baby?"

"Okay, I'll boil extra water, but I'll need to go to the artesian spring tomorrow to get more because I don't want to leave you right now," she called back.

And she couldn't go to the spring alone, or a tree, or elk, or whatever would try to kill her. But I didn't say that.

"Okaaaaahhhhh..." A contraction hit me midsentence and a growl ripped from my throat.

Motherfucker, this hurt way worse than I thought it would. How had this happened so fast? Didn't women labor for like hours? I mean, I was having that rock-hard belly and cramping all day, but that hadn't been labor, right?

"I feel like I have to poop!" I yelled, and Sage rushed into the room wide-eyed.

Her hands were scrubbed clean and dripping wet.

"Are you sure, or are you going to go poop outside and a baby is going to pop out?"

My eyes widened at the thought.

"Oh God, don't scare meeeahhhh!" Another contraction hit me and the urge to poop or push consumed me.

"Screw the shower, Sage. I think the baby is coming," I said through gritted teeth.

Sage ran forward as I popped onto all fours and she positioned herself behind me like she was going to catch a football. "Ohmygod, I see some brown baby head hair!" Sage screamed.

Shock ripped through me at that. "How is this happening so fast?" I asked, before another contraction hit. When I yelled, Sage told me to push.

I did, and my entire vagina felt like it split open. Red hot pain sliced between my legs so fast I felt like I was going to pass out.

"Shifter births are quicker, I think. My mom said something about it, but I never listened" was all Sage offered. "She's stuck halfway, Demi. I can see the tip of her ear. I need one more push and I can pull her out."

The pain was unbearable, so much so that my legs shook and I wanted to pass out. I burst into sobs. This was too hard. It hurt too much and I wanted Sawyer here. I wanted my mom, I wanted a fucking epidural.

"I can't," I whimpered. "It hurts."

"Demi Calloway-Hudson, you are the strongest woman I know. You can *absolutely* do this!" Sage yelled.

My belly seized up again as the pain of another contraction hit me, and I held my breath, pushing with everything I had.

I pushed so hard, I was sure I was going to push out my organs! There was a searing pain, like someone had lit my vagina on fire, and then a giant relief. I collapsed to the ground, trembling as the throbbing between my legs lessened.

"It's a...boy," Sage said beside me, and then burst into tears. "A beautiful boy, Demi. You did it!"

I rolled onto my back as I burst into sobs. My eyes searched the space until they landed on Sage and the naked flailing baby in her arms.

He let loose with a big cry, and Sage and I both erupted into relieved laughing.

I did it!

Reaching out, she laid him on my bare chest, and I peered down into his deep blue eyes. Seeing those eyes, his tiny perfect button nose, and thick mop of dark brown hair, it formed a sob in my throat. He looked *just* like his dad. I'd stopped reliving the memories of Sawyer in my head the past few months; they were too painful. Sawyer the day I met him at Delphi, Sawyer when he proposed, Sawyer kissing me. Now all of those memories came rushing back and my unbridled joy was mixed with a deep yearning for this baby to know his father, for Sawyer to see what perfect creature we'd created.

"Oh my God, he's a mini Sawyer." Sage knelt on the ground with me and looked down at him. "Crap, we didn't brainstorm boy names!"

I chuckled, looking into those deep blue eyes as he searched mine curiously. "Creek Curt Calloway-Hudson."

Tears ran down my face in thin rivulets as baby Creek started to make an O with his mouth, before finding my nipple.

"I think that's a perfect name." Sage's voice was thick with emotion. "Also, I never thought I would say this, but I'm going to get the placenta bowl."

I burst into laughter, and Sage did too. I was so glad she was here. What a gift loyal and true friends were.

I grinned, looking down at my perfect baby boy. "Your auntie Sage is a little wild but you're going to love her."

I placed a kiss on his soft head, and he clamped a hand around my finger. My heart throbbed in that moment because Sawyer should be here. This was so beautiful. I couldn't imagine raising this child without my mate.

"We're going to find Daddy, okay? Don't worry," I told Creek, and then the exhaustion pulled at my limbs, and I lay my head back to rest.

CHAPTER TEN

Three months later...

I DIDN'T KNOW WHETHER TO CELEBRATE BEING HERE one year or cry. Baby Creek was three months old and could now hold his head up, so we didn't need to worry about the floppy neck he'd had the first two months. I was sleep-deprived as all hell, but Sage was such a huge help. Sometimes I just woke up in the middle of the night and Sage was holding the baby to my chest so he could breastfeed; then she would change him and put him back in his bassinet.

We'd made some tightly packed cotton diaper pouches, but mostly we let him be naked and tried to take him outside often to pee or poo. I was probably completely psychologically damaging him by treating him like a dog in potty training, but we were doing the best we could. Slipping Creek into the carrier Sage had made me, I stepped outside to find her.

She was washing some tubers outside in a large clay pot. We knew nothing about when to feed a baby food, but baby Creek had started grabbing for our food at mealtimes, so we'd decided to try some mashed potatoes today.

"Hey, I was thinking of meditating for a bit; do you mind looking after him?" I asked Sage. "He's just fed."

Her hair was waist-length and braided into a thick red rope at her back. When she looked up at me, she smiled. "Absolutely. Come to Auntie, sunshine." She dropped the tubers and held out her arms.

I quickly unslung him and handed him off. "Thanks."

I'd been searching for a deeper meaning to everything lately. The universe, God, whatever Astra believed, something that would give order or meaning to my life in the grander picture. I just felt like there was a missing piece here and that it might be something spiritual within me that was broken and needed fixing. I began the meditation a week after baby Creek was born and I'd been doing it daily ever since. It helped with my stress of not being able to get back home, and the feelings of hopelessness quickly eased.

Today, I was going to search deep within myself and ask myself *what* I still needed to trust, because now that I had Creek, I couldn't imagine raising him without his father and grandparents. And I missed my pack: Astra, Arrow, Willow, and even Rab. Today I would start cave hunting again on a daily basis until we got out of here.

Stepping away from Sage and the baby, I walked to the edge of our little meadow and sat down on the smooth, flat rock that overlooked the steep embankment that led to the trickling creek, the creek I'd named my son after.

One year. One year ago today, I'd entered the woods for my alpha trial... I'd told Sawyer I would see him in three days. I'd said *three days* and it had been a *year*.

Willow's baby. The Paladin land. I'd ruined everything.

A sob formed in my throat but I swallowed it down. Now was not the time to be emotional. I'd spent a year having a pity party for myself. Now was the time to suck it up and get out of here.

Closing my eyes, I took in a deep cleansing breath through my nose and then exhaled through my mouth. The bubbling sounds of the creek water coupled with the rustling of the leaves put me into a calm state.

Plain as day once you trust.

The words of my ancestors looped in my head.

I found it. Trust. Plain as day. Trust, trust, trust.

I'd had a thought late last night. What if the trust was different for each alpha? What if Run never trusted the land, or his own heart, or something like that? What if each alpha had an issue trusting something in life and coming out here forced you to confront that?

Chills ran the length of my arms at the rightness of that thought.

Run loved my mom, that much was clear, but did he struggle with that love of a city girl? Did *that* stick him here for three years? Did he feel something was wrong with him for loving the enemy?

A great wind ripped through the canyon then; the leaves rustled as if trying to speak to me.

I breathed in slowly, feeling closer than ever to figuring this out.

"What don't *I* trust?" I whispered out loud.

I trusted my heart, my love for Sawyer, this land that had kept me alive for years. I trusted all of that.

'*Yourself,*' my wolf whispered softly, startling me. '*Your body.*'

My throat tightened as images of my rape flashed through my mind. Silk sheets, muffled screams, blackness.

Shame. Defeat. Betrayal. Weakness.

The sob that bubbled to the surface now was too big to gulp down, so I opened my mouth and let it rip out of me as it transformed into a howl.

My wolf was right...

I'd stopped trusting my body the night I was raped. I was ashamed I couldn't protect myself, ashamed I didn't scream louder or fight harder. Ashamed that I didn't do more to get Vicon arrested, although I *knew* that wasn't true, that I wasn't in the wrong and had nothing to be ashamed of.

When I couldn't protect myself, my soul split in two and my wolf had to protect us, had to be the badass, the strong one, the one I could always rely on when things got tough.

But hadn't I just survived out here in the middle of the freaking woods with bears and the threat of starvation and pregnancy...all on my own? My wolf was with me yes, but she'd barely done anything to help out here. *I* fetched the water, *I* hiked the mountain, *I* hunted the meals, *I* built the addition to the cabin with my strong hands. *I* pushed a baby out of my damn vagina with no pain meds, not my wolf.

I was a badass and I needed to trust myself. This human part of Demi was *anything* but weak. *Anything* but full of shame.

Tears flowed down my cheeks as my throat tightened with emotion. "I trust myself," I whispered.

"I trust my body." I broke into a sob, my throat tightening to the point of pain as I tried to hold back my tears.

Something inside of me mended itself then. I couldn't say exactly what it was, but it fused together in that moment...a rightness, an effervescent filling up the darkest part of my soul. I could trust myself to get us out of here. Just because my wolf and I were split didn't mean we weren't the same.

I was her; she was me. We were one. I saved myself that day with Vicon, and I was going to get us home now. Today.

My eyelids snapped open and I jumped up from where I sat.

"Sage!" I yelled, running full speed to where she was cutting the tubers with baby Creek on her back.

She looked up at me in alarm.

"I'm going to find the cave. Right now. I know where it is," I told her. I didn't actually know, but I knew it would reveal itself to me. I *felt* it.

True to our promise, I hadn't gone looking for three months; I'd just spent time figuring this whole mom thing out.

She stilled, hands shaking slightly. "Did you?"

"Trust myself!" I burst into tears. "I needed to learn that I could trust myself to protect my body. Something I was never able to do when I was fifteen because of my attack."

Sage dropped the knife, tears forming in her eyes as she nodded. Stepping over the pile of diced tubers, she opened her arms and pulled me into a hug. My face leaned over her shoulder, and then I was staring into the deep blue eyes of my baby.

This baby needed his dad. We needed to be a family. I needed Sawyer.

"Mommy's going to get us home, okay, baby?" I told him.

This was the only home he'd ever known, but I wanted so much more for him.

My parents needed to meet him. Raven. *Sawyer.* I wanted my family.

Baby Creek blew spit bubbles with his mouth, giving

me a gummy grin, and I pulled back from Sage. "Let's go together, and then when I find the cave, you can wait outside with Creek?"

I didn't want her attacked while I was gone. These woods were constantly trying to kill her if I wasn't nearby.

She nodded. "Okay...you seem really sure..."

There was such a knowing inside of me—I just couldn't explain it. "Sage, we're going home. Today."

Her eyes filled with more tears, and I walked into the cabin, grabbing a black chalk stick and writing an addition to the sentence that I had plastered on the wall. One day Creek might be out here, and he would find this.

Trust yourself, your heart, the land, whatever it is that is broken inside of you. Make peace with that and fully trust it, and the cave will show itself to you.

Throwing dirt on the fire, I watched as the smoke rose into the chimney in long curling tendrils.

Sage stepped beside me and we looked at our small space.

Home.

"This is goodbye," I told the small mud-plastered walls that I had insulated with my bare hands. Together, Sage and I quickly tidied up and prepared to leave our life here. I grabbed a sheepskin blanket in case the temperature dropped tonight and we were still finding our way out, but I left almost everything else. Anything left behind was something that would benefit my future children, and their children when they came out here.

We filled our canteens with water and tossed the rest from our storage pot so that it wouldn't mold. I grabbed the clay rattle Sage had made baby Creek, and then we left.

Placing one hand on the side of the house, I took in a deep breath. "Thank you."

I would miss this place. As hard as it was here, it was a simple life, and I found a part of myself I didn't know was missing in this cabin. A strong woman who could do anything. A leader. An alpha. A mother. A flawed but fierce woman who could survive hell and back.

CHAPTER ELEVEN

IT WAS A STRENUOUS HIKE UP THE MOUNTAIN. I WAS still in the best shape of my life, but having the baby and then taking three months off from my usual daily hiking regimen had dulled my stamina. Not to mention I was running on three hours of sleep because baby Creek was going through a growth spurt or something. He wanted to eat like every hour throughout the night. It was exhausting.

But we made it to the top.

Taking a water break, Sage and I panted while Creek slept in the sling around my shoulders.

"I'll take him now," Sage whispered, and I nodded gratefully. I needed to start scouting for the cave, although something told me it would be easy now.

My wolf surged to the surface, ready to do the thing where we split up, but I stopped her.

'*Let's do this together. As one,*' I told her, and felt her acceptance and pride at that decision.

I trust myself.

Purely on instinct, I set off to the right and started my hike to the top, just trusting that I would find it on the way. Sage and the baby followed at a good distance behind me, giving me the space to sense and feel what I needed to. I scanned the mountain wall to my left with a critical eye, looking for grooves or holes or something that might have suddenly appeared that I might have missed before.

Then I felt it.

The cold breeze, the smell of magic.

It was the same spot I'd sensed something in before. Taking a few more steps toward the steep mountain, I could see where new grass had grown over the spot I'd clawed at. The blades were shorter than the grass around it. The closer I got, the more the air felt heavy and the hair on my arms rose with electricity.

'*Trust,*' my wolf whispered.

This was it. My instincts had led me there before and here I was again.

Taking in a deep breath, I looked back at Sage and my sweet baby boy, nodded once, and stepped forward, walking straight into the mountain with complete faith that I had found the Cave of Magic and that whatever lay inside was something I could handle. One step, two, three, when I got within six inches of the dirt wall, it began to...flicker. Like a mirage, it became wavy and then transparent, before disappearing completely and revealing a deep black open tunnel straight into the mountain.

Sage gasped behind me, and a tear slid down my cheek as the relief of an entire year's worth of searching culminated in this one moment.

"I'll be right back," I told Sage without looking over my shoulder. I walked straight into the darkness. Blue flames flared to life at my sides simultaneously, causing me to jump a little.

I got this. I was made for this. I'm ready. I had to talk myself through it.

As I stepped deeper into the cave, the temperature dropped and the smell of magic became pungent. I could nearly taste it, like hot metal and electricity. Astra never actually told me what I would find in this cave or what I was really going to do when I got here.

With each step, more lanterns lit, until a faint blue glow flickered in the very center.

Steeling my breath, I walked into the large opening, toward the blue light.

Holy mother of shifters.

The tunnel had opened up into a giant cavern, too tall and too wide for my brain to fathom. The entire mountain must be hollow...

The sides of the walls were filled with rich green creeping vines and brilliantly colored flowers. Around the border of the space was a ring of weeping willows that glowed with the vibrant blue hue that lit up the entire space. These trees, this place, it was...magic.

My skin buzzed with electricity as my wolf came closer to the surface out of curiosity. Following a stony path, I walked through the outer ring of glowing weeping willows and into the center of the mountain. It was a good ten minute walk through a legit fairy-tale garden. The white crushed-stone path glowed supernaturally as it led me weaving in and out of vibrant ferns and wild dandelions, all growing out of a bright green bed of moss. I ducked under vines and trees until finally I reached an opening that seemed to be in the center of the mountain.

There, in the middle of the mossy ground, was a flat stone tablet.

I stared at the sentence engraved on the stone and squirmed, scared to read it aloud. But I knew I must. I'd come all this way, been through too much to turn back now.

I also noticed an engraved handprint underneath, where I assumed I was supposed to put my hand. My eyes skimmed over the words as I prepared to say them aloud.

I, NAME, give everything that I am to this land and to my people, and I pray that I be found worthy of leading them.

What if I'm not found worthy? What will happen? Will I never make it home?

Only one way to find out. With a final gulp, I bent on one knee before the gray stone tablet and placed my hand over the impression.

"I, Demi Spirit Moon Calloway-Hudson, give everything that I am to this land and to my people, and I pray that I be found worthy of leading them," I said with a healthy mixture of confidence and fear.

The moment the final word left my lips, an electrical jolt shot up my arm and into my body. I was thrown backward as the blue light from the willow trees suddenly snaked out in long thin strands and wrapped around me, lifting me into the air.

I gasped then as I felt the consciousness of thousands of people merge with mine.

'Alpha,' I heard Astra whimper.

'Alpha,' Rab huffed in awe.

I felt Willow and Arrow and all the other Paladins, most of whose names I didn't even know yet. I felt their love for their people, their land, love for me, and it filled me up until every corner of my soul was completely void of loneliness.

Tears trickled down my cheeks as my wolf howled inside of me.

'I'm coming home,' I told them.

Still suspended in midair, there was a pulse, a knocking against my sternum, and then more connections invaded my consciousness. Water, trees, soil, it was all alive. The Paladin land was special. It was linked to this cave and I knew that now. The Dark Woods were sacred, only for alphas, and Sage's presence here was not allowed. It was like the trees were talking to me, telling me all of this.

I mentally sent an *I'm sorry for Sage being here*, and then the magic set me back down and released its wisps from my body.

Something flickered before me, and I blinked rapidly to make sure I wasn't losing my mind.

The ghost of a man stood before me. He was tall, with long silky brown hair. When I studied the shape of his face, my jaw opened in shock...I looked like him.

Running Spirit.

He smiled at me, bowing his head deeply before another flicker of light shimmered to his left and Red Moon popped into view. The old man who had saved me from my fall at the base of Waterfall Mountain looked ten years younger as he beamed down at me and bowed deeply. Another flicker, and then another, as all of my ancestors appeared and each bowed to me before they started to walk in a circle around me. I wept as the emotions all became too much. Everything around me spun as dizziness washed over me. The spirits of my ancestors started to fade and I wiped away my tears.

"Thank you," I croaked, while the room spun harder, and I wondered if I was going to pass out. There was a popping noise, and then I blinked, confused.

What the...?

I was at the top of the mountain now...standing in front of the large wooden tree trunk with all of the previous names engraved in the rough-hewn bark.

Was the cave...a portal? I shivered at the thought. That had been some crazy stuff down there. The magic, feeling Rab and Astra, and then seeing Red and everyone. I did it...I felt my pack, my land, everything. I was their alpha. The trial was over and I was found worthy.

I needed to get back to Sage and Creek, but I knew there was one last thing to do. Bending down, I pulled my hunting knife from my belt and finished carving my name. I'd started the *D* all those months ago, but knowing it felt wrong I'd stopped, sensing it was something all of the others did only when they had completed their time here.

Demi Spirit Moon. When I was finished, I sat back and observed my accomplishment.

I did it. I found the cave. I was found worthy. Now I got to go home. Tears streamed down my face as I placed my hand on the flat wood and caressed each name of my ancestors.

"Goodbye. Thank you," I murmured as I stood, preparing to make my way back down the mountain. Then I heard a very distinctive sound.

A wolf's growl.

More specifically, *Sage's* wolf's growl.

"I'm coming!" I took off down the mountain, veering down the path that would hopefully lead me to them.

Why was Sage in wolf form? If she was a wolf, where the hell was my baby? As I ran, my own wolf surged to the surface, leaping out of my body and solidifying in front of me. I nearly toppled off the side of the cliff as I ran vampire fast, until I skidded to a stop behind the giant black bear, who reared up on his hind legs and roared.

My breath caught in my throat. He was about to slam down on Sage's small wolf, Sage who stood protectively over my sleeping baby with her lips peeled back in a snarl.

'STOP!' I mentally commanded the bear, throwing my hands forward. An unseen force slammed into the giant beast. He shook and then froze, giving Sage's wolf enough time to grab the cloth of the shoulder sling and drag my sleeping Creek out of harm's way. The bear was frozen, standing in an awkward position, and I wondered if I'd done that. I took two steps until I was facing him, and shock ripped through me to find him *literally* frozen. His eyes moved frantically left and right, but his mouth was unmoving, open in a roar, his paws stuck in midair.

I'd told him to stop...but I didn't think... *Whoa*. Was this some new Paladin alpha power? Or one I'd always had and never knew about?

Then I heard the most beautiful sound in the world. *The drums.*

The Paladin drums that would lead us home.

"I said I'm sorry for having Sage here! Now we're leaving and I don't want any more trouble while I escort her out of the sacred woods," I told the bear, the trees, and whoever else was listening.

'Go!' I shouted, and the bear slammed down onto all four paws and took off running up the mountain and away from us.

When I turned back around, Sage was back in her human form, dressed and cradling my baby to her chest.

"I take it you found the cave?" She looked wide-eyed at the bear now fleeing us.

I nodded, the beat of the drums so loud it practically vibrated my entire body. "And that's our way out. Come on!"

Sage frowned confusedly, looking at the direction I pointed.

I stopped. "The drums, don't you hear them?"

Her frown grew deeper as she shook her head.

Hmm, must be a Paladin thing.

She handed Creek to me, and in one quick move, I slung him over my chest before looping my arm through Sage's.

"Let's go home," I told her.

She seemed unsure, as if she didn't want to put hope in something that wasn't going to pan out. But I'd never been surer of anything. I could feel them—my pack, my people, my land. The Paladins were waiting for me. Pulling her forward, I forced her to take the first few steps until finally she started to quickly walk in stride with me.

"We're going home?" Sage seemed like she was in shock. The beating of the drums grew louder with each step away from the mountain.

I nodded. "Home to potato chips, cupcakes, and makeup!" I grinned.

A smile finally tugged at Sage's lips. "I just can't wait to shave my legs."

We both burst into laughter as I led her forward. The trees had parted in such a way that a path had formed.

"Manis and pedis!" Sage screamed out in joy.

"TV and air-conditioning!" I shouted.

"Pillow-top mattresses!"

"Underwear!"

"Shampoo!"

"Salt!"

"Ranch dressing!"

I burst out laughing.

"Instagram!"

"Shopping!" Sage cried out.

"Sawyer..." My voice lowered in reverence as I realized what this meant. I was finally going home to him.

Sage nodded. "Walsh too. Boys in general, really. I can't wait to get laid."

I threw my head back and laughed throatily. Good thing the baby was too young to know what that meant.

The trees had rearranged themselves to create a four-foot-wide trail right down the mountain, clearly a path the woods had made to lead us home, and we were going as fast as we could without tripping.

"It's been a year," I said, almost speaking to myself. "What if...?"

"It'll be fine. Whatever it is, we can deal with it together."

I could sense Astra, Willow, Rab, and the others were alive, but not how they felt or where exactly they were. These conscious threads binding me to them were new to me, and I was still trying to figure them out.

When I recognized the section of the woods we'd just stepped through, I nearly burst into a sob. The trees were thinning, and the bronze plaque that warned of the danger of the Dark Woods glinted in the fading light.

"We made it!" I cried, and the drums beat louder as if whoever was pounding on them sensed my closeness.

Running full throttle now, tears streaming down both of our faces, I passed the Paladin farmlands, still black from disease—but a few new green buds had formed from the looks of them. Whatever had happened in the cave had worked! We ran harder, coming into town.

That's when I noticed something was wrong. The buildings didn't look right. The blackness wasn't disease... It was...soot, like they'd been burned. Some of them were half caved in.

I skidded to a stop, just in time to see half a dozen

Ithaki step out from behind a shelled-out Paladin home. They were dragging a large cage behind them with some type of animal inside. The sight of the Ithaki walking through Paladin Village made a growl rise in my throat. As they drew closer, my gaze fell onto what was inside the cage and a scream ripped from my throat.

Astra.

Underfed, dirty, and banging that little drum like her life depended on it. Her ankles were shackled, limp brown hair so long it was well past her shoulders. My heart nearly stopped right there at the sight of her. When she looked up at me, her hand froze in midair and a grin swept across her face. She looked so grown-up...but there was a darkness in her blue eyes that hadn't been there before. They'd broken her, taken her innocence.

Motherfuckers.

"Ahh, the demon has finally shown up," one of the Ithaki said, holding a long whip in his hand. Another half dozen Ithaki stepped out behind them, and I knew I wasn't getting Astra out of that cage without a fight.

Unbridled rage surged up inside of me as I slowly unslung baby Creek and handed him to Sage. "Go to the bunker," I said through clenched teeth. "I'll meet you there. Get him safely inside."

Sage's eyes widened as she took the baby. "No way. I'm not leaving you to fight alon—"

"Run, and don't stop until you reach the bunker under the school," I ordered her.

"No," Sage growled, her eyes going yellow as she looked at the dozen Ithaki now pulling weapons from behind their backs.

"*Yes,*" I growled. "I need to know Creek is safe or I can't fight properly," I told her. "I need you to trust me, Sage. Everything is different now. That cave changed me. I'll kill every single one of these motherfuckers before they lay a finger on me or Astra."

She eyed the dozen Ithaki behind me, who had now started to advance with weapons drawn.

"You *sure* you have enough power to fight them all?"

I grinned, magic coursing through my veins stronger than ever before.

"They'll wish they never laid a hand on Astra." Then I quickly kissed Creek's soft head. "Mommy loves you."

With a final nod, Sage took off running.

I wasn't worried about her ability to take care of herself or my baby now that she was out of the cursed woods. Sage was a badass who wouldn't stop until Creek was safe in the bunker with Sawyer. But I wasn't leaving here without Astra.

No way in hell.

"Let her go and I won't kill you," I calmly told the Ithaki as magic built up inside of me.

They burst into laughter, looking at each other with wide expressions like I must be joking.

Astra peered up at me, collapsing back into the

cage in exhaustion, her little drum falling at her feet. Something dark and feral snapped inside of me.

I thrust my hands out, sending a shock wave of energy at the group of Ithaki. Their bodies blew backward as if they'd been hit by a car, and I kicked off the ground, running right at them with vampire speed. The first one looked up at me with wide terrified eyes and pointed ears right as I put my hunting blade to his neck and dragged it across his throat, before moving to the next.

My time in the Dark Woods had taught me that there was no joy in watching an animal have a slow torturous death. Whether it be a rabbit or a deer, I always made sure to make their end as quick and painless as possible. But for these monsters, I wanted to carve their insides out before their watching eyes, but there was no time.

Leaping to the next fallen man, I cut his throat too. At the same time, I kept whatever power I'd thrown over the Ithaki pressed down upon them so that they were essentially pinned to the dirt, waiting for death.

How dare they cage Astra like an animal? *How fucking dare they?!* I leaped from body to body in a blind rage, using my vampire speed. When I reached the last one, a female, she was crying, bucking against the invisible restraints I held over her. She looked up at me with tears in her eyes.

"Please," she croaked. "Have mercy. I have a child."

The unbridled rage fueling my murder-fest left me like a popped balloon.

She was a mother...

With the absence of my rage also came the absence of my power over her. The second I freed her magical restraints, she lurched forward and slammed her forehead into my nose.

Pain exploded between my eyes as blood spurted over my face in a gush. Blurry tears swam in my vision, and dizziness washed over me as I fell backward off of her and she scrambled to get up.

"Look out!" Astra screamed.

Everything was blurry as I blinked back the tears to clear my vision, just in time to see the Ithaki woman charging me with a knife. My wolf surged to the surface, leaping out of my chest and coming at the woman before I could even respond.

"What the fu—" The woman's shout of alarm turned into a wet gurgle as my wolf snapped for her throat, ripping it clean out.

Now that the threats were gone, I scrambled forward and knelt before the cage, my fingers gripping the bars until my knuckles turned white. My wolf leaped back into my body, giving me strength as I peered at Astra.

"Alpha, you came." Astra smiled at me with her little dirt-caked cheeks.

I was so overcome with emotion that I couldn't speak for a moment. "I heard your drums."

"You had a baby." Astra grinned, looking out of it and spacy. Her voice was weak and breathy.

Not wanting her to spend another second in this cage, I ripped outward until the entire door came off in my hands.

"I did have a baby," I told her, reaching in the cage to pull her fragile body out. She was too light. Oh God, what had they done to her? "You want to meet him?" I looked down at her as she smiled up at me. "Come on." I heaved her into a standing position but her legs collapsed.

"I can't walk." Astra frowned. "They...didn't like it when I played the drum."

A sob formed in my throat, but I swallowed it down. "They're gone now. No one is going to hurt you ever again. I'm so sorry I failed to protect you." I wept freely now, no longer trying to hide my emotions from her, no longer able to.

Astra reached up and cupped my chin gently. "You did it. Like I knew you would." She went cross-eyed and her fingers fell away from my face.

Horror seized me and I shook her.

"Astra! Look at me!" I scooped her in my arms, realizing that she was near death. Running past Rab's old house, now nearly leveled to the ground, I burst into the old birthing center, taking cover in case there were more Ithaki patrolling this place.

I'd been gone a year. I had no idea what the new rules and territories were. But from the looks of the ragtag group that had greeted me and the blackened crops when I'd come in, this place wasn't exactly habitable.

I pulled out my water canteen and popped off the cap, putting it to her lips. When I tipped it back, she gulped it greedily, something coming alive in her gaze.

That's it. Fight.

Next, I pulled out the last two pieces of smoked rabbit meat I had and gave them to her. Her hands shook as she shoved them in her mouth, chewing ferociously.

Were they starving her? Fresh rage boiled inside of me, but I shoved it down.

"There you go. You're okay now." I smoothed her hair, which felt matted, and I had to swallow down my anger even more lest it blind my ability to properly care for her.

"I've been gone a year... Can you tell me what happened?" I asked her, wondering if she was aware enough to tell me what had gone down in my absence.

She grabbed my canteen, drinking more water to wash down the final hunk of rabbit, and then nodded.

"A week after you left, Sage went looking for you. A week after that, the Ithaki raided the village. Rab and a small contingent of others fought, but..." Her eyes dropped to the ground.

"But what?" My body stilled.

She swallowed hard. "But a lot died. And then Rab made the call to get everyone else in the bunker. He forced me to go too, but I ran away before they went in, came back to play the drum and wait for you."

My heart couldn't take much more. "Astra, you didn't need to do that. I—"

She reached out and grasped my hand in a frail grip. "I wasn't going to let you be lost forever. To come back to nothing."

I leaned forward, pulling her into a hug, and we just held each other for a few long moments.

"Thank you," I whispered as we finally pulled back.

She bowed her head deeply. "It's been my pleasure, Alpha."

This world didn't deserve such an innocent and loyal person. *I* didn't deserve her. Astra was a Paladin national treasure that needed to be protected at all costs from now on.

"You want to go find the others now?" I asked with a slight smile. "I think it's time we reunited the pack."

Astra grinned, and I stood. She tried to stand too, but her legs gave out and I caught her by the elbow. "I can't walk," she whimpered.

"Then I'll carry you," I told her, and lifted her into my arms. It was the least I could do after everything she'd done for me. Slipping out the front door, I moved to leave the building when Astra stopped me.

"Wait." She reached out and grabbed a little glass jar.

I thought it might be food and was grateful she would have more since she clearly needed like two-foot-long subs right now, but when she opened it, I recognized the blue paint inside.

She dipped her finger into the jar and traced a line with her pinky from the bottom of my lip to the tip of my chin. Then she did two small lines under each of my eyes, and two dots under those.

"Now we're ready, Alpha," she told me. I looked up at a reflective metal plate that hung on the wall and was shocked at the woman staring back at me.

I hadn't seen my reflection for a year. Well, not in a mirror.

The blood from when the Ithaki bashed my nose covered my upper lip and chin, coupled with the bright blue paint, and a wild and fierce look in my deep cobalt eyes. I looked like...a female you did *not* want to fuck with.

Turning back to the open doorway, with Astra cradled in my arms, I stepped out into the open air and gasped at what I saw.

"See? You did it." Astra gleamed as we both stared at the rich and restored land. The once dry and blackened grass that had covered the village was now a vibrant green. Ferns, junipers, oak trees, all of their leaves were rich and alive. Green vines began to grow right before our eyes, creeping along the trellis that hung above the entrance to the birthing center.

The land could grow crops now; we could fix up the buildings and move everyone back. Joy spread throughout my limbs at the sight of the reward of everything I went through over the last year...but I didn't have time to hang back and see the land restore itself.

I needed to see Sawyer.

'Sawyer!' I tried, realizing that a year without mentally

speaking to my mate and husband had made me forget that I could.

I ran across the main road of the Paladin village with Astra in my arms and waited for a reply.

'Sawyer, I made it back! Where are you?'

There was no response. I frowned as I snaked through the village, trying to not be seen in case there were any lingering Ithaki.

Maybe he couldn't communicate so deep underground in the bunker?

"Most of the Ithaki left after they realized the land was dead," Astra told me softly.

I nodded, running out into the open now that I knew no more Ithaki were likely to be here. "Do you know what became of Wolf City?" I chewed on my lip, panting as I ran, trying not to jostle Astra. She was heavier than Creek obviously, but still way too light. I was going to watch her eat five platefuls of food once we settled in the bunker with everyone.

Astra shook her head. "Just that it's common ground now. All vampires, witches, fey, and trolls are allowed to live there and take what they want from there."

My body seized at her words, and I had to consciously be aware not to squeeze her too tightly in my anger.

Common ground. One of the most territorial species on the planet now had their homeland shared by all?

Over my dead fucking body.

I pumped my legs, putting my feelers out there to try

and make sense of these bonds and ties I was sensing. Rab, Arrow, Willow, Luna, Crescent, names I didn't even know prior to today but now I *knew* that person, I knew they were pack. They were family. *Mine.*

Taking a deep breath, I focused on Rab. He felt strong, healthy, a little down, but okay.

'You did it.' Rab's voice suddenly boomed in my head and I faltered, nearly tripping over my own feet.

'Rab!'

'Alpha.'

A whimper left my throat at his declaration, the respect in his voice.

'I told you I would make it, you bastard,' I teased. *'Hey, how can we talk?'*

'You're my alpha. I'm pack. You can speak into any Paladin's mind you want now, and them into yours.'

Whoa. Like a real wolf pack... Sawyer couldn't do that.

'Did Sage make it to the bunker? Is that where you are? Are she and my baby safe?'

I had to slow down. I was getting winded.

'Yes. She said you were on your way with Astra. Gave us all a shock coming in with a baby... Congrats.'

I chuckled. Yeah, it was weird, I'd give him that. *'Thanks, are my parents okay? Sawyer? Is he happy about the baby?'*

Truth be told, I was a bit nervous to just drop the I-had-your-baby-in-the-woods on my husband.

'Everything is fine down here, but it's not safe for

181

you to just barge into Wolf City. I'm coming with Arrow to meet you at the border and sneak you in.'

I nodded, but something he said didn't add up.

Rab and Arrow were coming out to meet me, not Sawyer. There was no reality in which Sawyer would know I was back and not come out to meet me. Unless maybe he was with the baby, but why could Rab answer me and not Sawyer?

'Rab...where is Sawyer?' I clutched Astra in my arms, noticing that she'd fallen asleep on my chest. Poor thing needed food and rest.

'Slight complication with that, but I'll explain everything when you get down here. Don't worry.'

Okay...as much as I wanted to push him, force him as his alpha to tell me, I also trusted him and he was being very nonchalant...so it couldn't be that bad.

Right?

Unless Sawyer was in a coma, nearly beaten to death, and that's why he couldn't answer me!

'Sawyer, I'm back,' I tried again, but got nothing, felt nothing. Our bond was completely shut down.

I realized then that I loved Sawyer so much it hurt. It had reached that point of no return, where if something catastrophic happened to him, I would never be the same. Shoving those negative thoughts down, I ran, scouting the woods for Ithaki or vampires.

'We are at the hedge that surrounds the school and touches the border,' Rab told me.

'Hey, Alpha,' Arrow chimed in, and I grinned.

'Hey, meet you soon,' I told Arrow.

Sterling Hill, or what was left of it, was always surrounded by large leafy green privacy hedges. They went on for as far as the eye could see around the multi-acre property. If they were hiding near there, then I'd know about where to meet them, assuming I remembered the way. I'd been running through the Wild Lands, parallel to Wolf City, but I was far enough in the woods that I couldn't really see where I was in relation to Wolf City. Had I passed Sawyer's parents' house yet? Or what was left of it? I felt like I'd been running forever with Astra in my arms. Deciding to risk cutting closer to have a peek, I slowed and peered through the trees. What I saw stole my breath.

I'd found Sterling Hill and…it was gone. All of it. *Gone.*

The campus where I'd found my freedom, where I'd fallen in love with Sawyer, where I'd gotten to study photography, it was flattened. The only way I recognized it was from the position of the rubble and the parking lots and pathways.

Shadows walked along the paths, and I held my breath when I realized they were vampires. I could tell by the supernaturally fast way they walked. The sun was still high in the sky, which was typically vampire sleeping time. It meant they were taking caffeine pills to stay awake and patrol.

If they smelled me, or my power, we were screwed big ti—

"Alpha!" Rab whisper-screamed.

My head snapped to the hedge nearest me, and I broke into a run. Crossing through the final stretch of Wild Lands trees, I burst over the flag line and then out into the open for a split second before running vampire fast *into* the hedge.

I quickly learned the hedge was an illusion. It was hollow inside, with a chicken-wire cage. The hedge was actually creeper vines that grew around the cage so thickly you could barely see inside.

Genius. Whichever alpha had built the bunker had thought of everything, including this escape tunnel.

"Here you go." Rab held the cuffs Sawyer had given me as an engagement gift, and then took Astra from my arms, stroking her hair and face gently.

I'd forgotten about the cuffs. Seeing them gave me a visceral reaction at first, but then I reminded myself I could take them on and off at will. Slipping them on, I nodded to them.

"We tried to go back for her, snuck out many times, but—" Rab's voice croaked as he looked down at sleeping Astra in his arms.

I placed a hand on his shoulder. "It's okay. She needs some fluids and food, but she'll be okay."

Arrow bowed deeply to me, Rab did the same, clutching Astra to his chest.

"It's our honor to have you lead us, Alpha," Rab said.

Emotion clogged my throat. We were in a six-foot-tall, four-foot-wide hedge. This was not an ideal space for bowing, but they did it anyway.

"Thank you."

When they stood, they turned and started to walk deeper into the hedge, toward where I assumed the bunker was.

"Where is Sawyer?" I asked again, deciding this time to be more insistent no matter what he said.

"Shhh...will tell you inside. Vampires." Rab pointed to the hedge wall, and I chewed on my lip.

He was delaying...which meant it was bad.

If Sawyer was dead, I would feel it, right? I mean we were mates, imprinted. I would feel it...

Panic suddenly gripped me.

"He's alive, right?" I blurted out in a whisper-scream.

"He's alive," Arrow answered.

I nearly sagged with relief.

Then what's the big deal? I wanted to blurt out, but instead I followed them on through the tunnel. I just wanted to see my mom, and my baby, and Sawyer. We ran inside of the hollow hedge for what seemed like forever, until finally the boys stopped. There was a crouched figure up ahead, sitting cross-legged on the ground before a giant set of storm doors.

'How the hell did Sage find this place?' I asked Rab.

'We keep a scout out here twenty-four hours a day. She blew up a fey's car to create a distraction and the scout saw her and brought her in.'

Blew up a fey's car. That sounded like Sage.

I was just glad she and Creek were safe.

As we approached, the scout stood, and I was relieved to recognize someone. Quan, one of Sawyer's closest friends.

He nodded to me, and wordlessly opened the storm doors, careful to be as quiet as possible, to reveal a set of steep stairs.

As Arrow passed Quan, they did a bro fist bump and it warmed my heart to see the Paladin and city wolves working together so nicely. Rab looked back at me and caught me smiling at the two of them.

'Don't get excited. Not everyone here gets along. There have been fights to the death, and you are coming into an angry, hungry group of wolves who feel abandoned by their leaders. Prepare to prove yourself, Alpha.'

His words shocked the shit out of me.

Prove myself? I just fucking did that for the past year in the woods, alone. *Hungry?* Didn't they have enough food? Sawyer said there was enough for two years or something. I followed him down the steps, what must have been thirty feet, and the storm doors shut above us. When we reached the flat open room, two lights flickered on the walls to reveal a giant circular air lock.

I was still stuck on Rab's warning. Abandoned? He said the wolves felt abandoned by their leaders. "Wait, why would they feel abandoned? Sawyer has been here with them the whole time, right?"

Rab stopped, handing off Astra to Arrow. "Get her to medical," he said, and the vault door opened with a hiss. Through the crack in the door, I saw a giant concrete hallway. My mom held Creek, feeding him a bottle, and Sage had her arm around Raven. They were both talking to my dad, waiting to greet us.

A smile pulled at my mouth, and I went to step forward, forgetting all about my earlier question, when Rab stopped me, and let the vault door close again.

I looked up into his deep blue eyes and he took a steady breath. "Alpha, I regret to inform you—"

I put up a hand. "Don't be so formal with me, Rab. Just tell me. What happened to Sawyer?"

I steeled myself, preparing for some godawful news about my mate. He was paralyzed, maimed, kidnapped.

Rab swallowed hard. "A month after you left, Sawyer was found guilty of murdering the prince of Vampire City, Vicon Drake. He was captured and taken to Magic City Prison."

The room spun and I staggered backward as the air whooshed out of me. "No."

"You weren't there to testify to the claim of...sexual assault...and they had Sawyer's DNA all over the crime scene."

No! I broke down into sobs, my back slamming against the concrete wall as I slid into a sitting position. Sawyer, my Sawyer, in prison for almost a year because he was enacting justice on a sick soul and doing honor in *my* name. My breaths came out in short ragged gasps, and I knew I was on the verge of a full-blown panic attack.

Rab knelt down before me, meeting my gaze. "Now that you're back, we will figure this out."

I nodded, wiping my cheeks. "Where is Magic City Prison? Light Fey Territory?" I moved to stand and he backed up, putting his hands out.

"Yes, but—"

"I need to break him out. He's all alone in there, and—" Another sob threatened to take hold of me again.

Rab placed a hand on my shoulder. "We have serious issues you need to deal with here first. We're low on food. There was a mold contamination and we lost half of our supply early on. Also the air filter just broke, which we rely on for fresh oxygen. Then there is the issue with heating and cooling, which keeps going out. We need an exit plan, Demi. We can't live down here forever. People are getting stir-crazy and going topside and disappearing or winding up dead."

Oh God.

Okay. Focus, Demi. One thing at a time.

I shook my head to clear my thoughts. "The Paladin

land is healed. I saw it with my own eyes. You can move everyone there, rebuild and fortify the city while I go looking for Sawyer. I can't leave him in there alone."

"He's not alone," Rab told me. "The day after he got taken away, Walsh murdered the vampire king and then confessed to everything on tape so that he would be taken with Sawyer."

I blinked at him, stunned, unsure I'd heard him right. "Say what?"

Rab nodded. "The vampire king is dead. Only the queen is left and she rules everything. Walsh is with Sawyer in Magic City Prison so he can keep an eye on him."

Holy shit. Thank you, Walsh! That made me feel slightly better, but only slightly. Now I had two people to rescue.

Rab placed a hand on my shoulder. "Our people need to hear you tell them that the Paladin land is safe to go home to. That you found the cave and were found worthy and we can grow fresh food and prosper again. We need a leader."

He was right. Dammit, he was so right.

Okay.

I shook myself, preparing to live up to my promise and lead my people, lead Sawyer's people too, I guess. "Okay, a few days to sort things here, then I'm going to break Sawyer and Walsh out."

Rab nodded. "I heard your wolf can walk through

walls? Sounds like a handy trick when wanting to break into a prison."

I grinned as a calmness settled over me.

I was going to get my hubby back. We would have our happily-ever-after, damn it!

CHAPTER TWELVE

AFTER A FEW DEEP BREATHS, RAB OPENED THE STEEL vault door, and after a whoosh of air, I was welcomed by a small contingent of close friends and family. Raven, my parents, Sawyer's mom, Sage, the baby, Eugene, Arrow, Willow and her baby—they all stood smiling at me, and my heart felt so full in that moment I almost forgot about all of my troubles.

Almost.

"Alpha." Willow nodded, stepping forward, holding a baby girl who looked about six months old. I instantly smelled the humanness on her, and my heart pinched with regret.

"Willow, I'm so sor—"

"Isn't she perfect?" Willow smiled at me, stroking the baby's dark hair.

I caught myself. Why would I apologize for a healthy

human baby? There were plenty of people who would kill for one of those. As I stared at the child, I realized she was right. She was perfect. Ten fingers and ten toes. We'd been wrong before to worry about all the children born without wolves.

"She's absolutely perfect," I agreed, my throat tightening.

"And she'll have a playmate." Willow looked at my mom, who was watching me with eyes that brimmed over with tears.

"Oh, honey, you had a baby without me," my mom croaked, stepping forward. Sawyer's mom stood beside her. She was beaming as she looked down at Creek, who looked so much like Sawyer that it made me sad sometimes to look at him.

I rushed toward my mom, opening my arms and smooshing her in a hug. Creek was pressed between us, sucking the nipple of a plastic bottle and probably wondering what this plastic thing was. He'd never seen plastic. Or the white cotton diaper he was wearing, or the clean yellow onesie. He looked...like a city wolf. I'd enjoyed learning to live off the land, but something about disposable diapers just made everything seem right with the world.

Sawyer's mom stood near us, shifting awkwardly like she wanted to say something but wasn't sure what. Reaching one arm out, I pulled her into the hug with my mom, making it a three-way.

"I hope it's okay I gave him a bottle," my mom fumbled as she pulled back from our group hug. "He was crying and you weren't here and—"

I smiled. "It's fine. I'm just not used to diapers and clothes and stuff."

Wow, where had my social skills gone?

My mom looked at my skimpy suede dress, unshaven legs, and the hunting knife strapped to my thigh, and nodded. "Well, whatever you're comfortable with, dear. I can change him back into the rabbit fur if—"

I laughed, and so did Sage, who stood behind my mom. If I never had to skin another rabbit, it would be fine by me.

"Normal clothes are fine," I assured her. When the time was right, I would teach my baby to live off the land too, but some city luxuries were awesome to have in the meantime.

Sawyer's mom reached out and gently touched Creek's forehead. "I'll have to show you a baby picture of Sawyer. I grabbed a few before the evacuation..." She shook off the memory. "They look so much alike."

I nodded. "I'd like that. Also, I wanted to tell you. His full name is Creek *Curt* Calloway-Hudson."

Her breath hitched and then tears spilled over onto her cheeks. "I love that."

I smiled, trying to keep from crying myself. "It has a nice ring to it."

Without warning, she reached out and pulled me in

for another hug. "Sawyer always talked about having kids one day. He would be so proud."

Would be...

He wasn't gone yet. She'd already given up hope?

I nodded into her shoulder, trying not to get too emotional. It was all so overwhelming. "I'm going to get him back. Don't worry."

My dad had been silently watching me the entire time. "They say you're their alpha now?" He slung an arm around my mother, looking from Rab to Arrow. Poor guy seemed confused by the whole thing. Could I blame him?

Something stirred within me at my father's words.

Anger. Why?

Because I wasn't *just* the alpha of the Paladins. With Sawyer gone, I'd need to be the leader of both packs until he could return, something I didn't think they would like but was necessary.

"I'm everyone's alpha now, Dad." I tipped my chin up, and Eugene, who was standing next to my father, gave me a terrifying grin.

"Until Sawyer is back, I'm your alpha too, and I'm going to have to make some hard decisions so I can get us all out of here and back topside." Then I popped on my toes and kissed his stunned cheek. "Missed you, Dad."

My dad looked shocked at my declaration. My mom too. But I didn't care. That's the way things were going to be. We needed one leader to unite us all or there was no way we were going to survive and eventually take Wolf City back.

"I'm so glad you're okay," Raven squeaked beside me, and I yanked my bestie into a hug. When my arms wrapped around her, the earthy scent of magic and spell work surrounded me and I felt like I was home, back in my parents' apartment in Spokane while Raven and I giggled about cute boys at Delphi when we were thirteen.

"Missed you the most," I whispered.

I had barely seen my bestie since the day I left Delphi well over a year ago.

When we pulled apart, we both wiped at our eyes.

"You look badass and slightly horrifying, like you eat raw cockroaches for breakfast," she told me, which caused me to burst out laughing.

"Hey, if you're hungry enough…" I shrugged and she smiled.

Eugene was next, pulling me in for a big bear hug.

"Sorry I couldn't protect Sawyer better. They had a tracker on the ankle bracelet and he didn't want to lead them into the bunker. He also didn't want to leave you," he murmured in my ear.

My heart thumped against my chest at that. That was Sawyer, sacrificing for those he loved. "You did fine. We'll get him back. I have a plan." I didn't really have a plan, but I was going to get him back. *That* was the plan. At all costs.

He pulled away from me and nodded, but I could see the shame written on his face.

Rab came to my side. "So the rumor mill started the second that all of the Paladin felt you claim the magic. The city wolves want to speak with you...and they are not pleased."

Not pleased?

I looked down at my dirty unshaven legs, knowing I had blood on my chin from my broken nose, which seemed to have already healed, and as much as I wanted to shower right now, it might benefit me to be seen like this. You didn't fuck with people who looked like they'd just walked out of the bush and knew how to gut a bunny rabbit, right? Like Raven said, I looked like I ate cockroaches for breakfast. That was an advantage in my opinion.

"Lead the way," I told him.

Arrow flanked my left, Rab my right, and Sage stepped up behind me.

"Mom, can you watch baby Creek for a bit?"

She nodded, her eyes brimming with tears.

I gave her a small tired smile and followed Rab and Arrow. "Astra is getting treatment?" I asked Arrow.

He nodded. "Doctor says it's severe dehydration and malnutrition. It's keeping her from healing. She'll be good as new by tomorrow."

The tension I didn't realize I was holding relaxed a little then. We walked down a long hallway and Rab cleared his throat. "Alpha, you should know that the city wolves have been talking for some time about escaping Magic City altogether and going to live in the human world undercover."

Sage gasped behind me. "*Hugely* against the rules unless banished, and even then only in Delphi and restricted areas of Spokane."

I didn't know the rules but that sounded about right. We couldn't have thousands of wolves running around Washington State and beyond.

"Not to mention the humans in the supernatural hunter societies. They regulate that sort of thing," Rab agreed. "I have told them this and they don't care. They want fresh air and food."

Human hunters in the supernatural what now? I'd heard rumors of them at Delphi but had never seen one. They were some uber religious Catholic group who were hell-bent on wiping the "evil" out of the world. I thought they were a myth.

I tipped my chin to him. "And they'll get their fresh air and food. In Paladin Village, where we will all go together, as one pack."

Rab smirked, Arrow too.

I didn't care anymore about what anyone thought. The Dark Woods had freed me of all that shit. I wanted my people safe, and then I was going to get my man.

As we approached a large set of metal double doors that read *Mess Hall*, I could hear muffled shouting.

Taking a deep breath, I calmed myself and then nodded to Rab, who opened the door.

I was assaulted with a barrage of smells first: stale food, musty indoor wetness, and the general stench of too many people packed in one room. Then the sounds hit me. Angry screaming and yelling, mostly male voices, as I took in the scene before me.

There were thousands of people in this giant central room. It was a huge rectangle with a cafeteria kitchen on either side and an area where you slid your tray along to pick up food. Behind the glass were some workers wearing hairnets and serving what looked like gloppy, nasty food. The tables in the middle of the room were giant. Each one seating at least a hundred people.

They still hadn't noticed my entrance. "How many people do we have down here in the bunker?" I asked Rab.

"Roughly eight thousand Paladin, and about double that in city wolves."

That sounded like too little. Twenty-four thousand people. The rest must have died.

But I didn't have the heart to ask.

"We have four mess halls and we eat at staggered times," Rab informed me. "The bunker is three stories. Living on base level, eating and exercise and medical on midlevel where we are now, and offices and supplies and engineering on top level."

Wow.

"Is there a way I can speak to everyone?"

Rab nodded, walking over to the wall and punching in a code. It seemed he'd been given some kind of leader status here, and that made me proud. Probably Eugene's doing. Rab pulled a handheld PA mic off a hook on the wall and approached me.

"You're live throughout the entire bunker," he said, handing me the mic.

Say what now? Shit, I wasn't good at speeches. That was Sawyer's department.

I cleared my throat, watching people argue and scream at each other.

"Settle down!" I shouted boldly, and my voice projected throughout the speakers on the wall.

"I am Demi Spirit Moon Calloway-Hudson, Sawyer Hudson's wife and *your* new alpha," I declared confidently.

There was a ring of cheers from the Paladins present but mostly boos from the city wolves.

I ignored the boos. "I've just been debriefed on the situation here. And I'm proud to report that the Paladin village land has been healed and is free of enemies. We can escape there and set up a new temporary village for everyone while I go and get Sawyer and Walsh."

More cheers mixed with only a few boos.

"We will have fresh water, food, and air there...daily sunshine, and we can function as *one pack*." I yelled the last two words for emphasis.

Silence descended over the crowd. I wondered what the other people in this place were thinking, hearing my voice coming out of the wall and stating all of this.

A man who I didn't recognize stepped forward and sneered. He was a city wolf, about midthirties, and looked like he'd seen better days. He had that wild, don't-fuck-with-me look—shaved head, hooded gaze, and rough skin. "You left us in this concrete hell for a *year*, and Sawyer got dragged away for protecting *you*. So who says you're in charge now?" He spit on the floor at my feet, and Rab moved forward to probably punch him, but Sage held him back.

She knew I could handle this myself.

I had zero time or patience for this bullshit.

Reaching into the thigh holster on my leg, I pulled my blade and gave this bastard the wildest look I could muster.

"*I* say so. Your alpha's *wife*, the mother of his *child*." People gasped in surprise at that. "And if you have a problem with that, you can fight me. Winner takes the pack." Then I growled, low and with warning, and I knew my eyes had flashed yellow because my wolf was so close to the surface, I had to make an effort to restrain her.

The Paladin wolves in the room roared their approval, jumping up onto the tabletops or pounding their open palms on it like they were drums. The man's nostrils flared as he looked over my face and then he lowered his head in defeat. Maybe it was my confidence, maybe it was the fact that he didn't want to fight a woman, or maybe it was the wild look in my eye and blood on my face mixed with war paint, but the dude stepped back.

"There is no *one* pack!" someone cried from deep in the crowd. "There is *them* and us!" he roared and too many people cried out in approval of his comment for my liking.

Paladin wolves might be "wild" by city wolves' thinking, but I just didn't care—I liked being wild and knowing how to live off the land. I liked knowing how to catch and cut up my own food. I liked being alpha, and no one was taking from me what was rightfully mine. I'd worked too hard for it.

I stepped forward, holding the PA mic to my lips. "I just spent a *year* in the woods. Lost, living off the land. I gave birth to Sawyer's son out there with no hospital and no medication. I *gave* myself to that mountain, to the land, and to my people, and I was found *worthy* of being alpha, so I *dare* any one of you who disagrees with that choice to speak up now. You'll end up rotting in this underground tomb because anyone who leaves is leaving as a part of *my* pack!"

Then I dropped the mic into Rab's outstretched hand and the group went wild, chanting, "Alpha! Alpha! Alpha!"

Most of them did anyway—some were stonily silent. I knew it would take time for old ways of thinking to be broken down, but I wasn't going to have a mutiny on my hands. If anyone wanted to live topside and be offered protection and life at Paladin Village, they were going to play by my damn rules.

"Is there enough room for all of us there?" someone screamed out over the yelling. A female voice.

I yelled loudly so that my voice could carry across the entire space. "We will make room. The Paladins don't depend on grocery stores to feed them and construction companies to build their houses. We will widen the village and build more houses. We can extend the farm crops too. *Everyone* will have an equal part sharing jobs. And then when I get back with Sawyer, we will get Wolf City back too."

That brought a chorus of cheers from each side. I didn't know what they had been through in my absence, but I could see their faces now held something I was proud to give them.

Hope.

I looked at Rab and lowered my voice. "I need Eugene and you, and any other leaders, in a room for war council briefing. But first I want to shower."

He nodded and we left the room as they were still cheering. I'd been stuck in the woods for a year and they'd been stuck down here. It was very much the same type of situation, and I was about to liberate them and bring them home.

Then I was focusing all of my energy on getting Sawyer and Walsh out of prison.

We exited the mess hall, and my mom and Raven were there holding and cooing at Creek. I slowed my approach and my mom held him out to me. Taking him in my arms, I gave him a little snuggle and kissed the top of his head. He craned his neck into my chest, searching for my boobs. My boobs hurt; they felt rock-hard, full of milk, and I knew nothing about how to dry them out, but I did know that I was raised on formula and I turned out okay. If I wanted to go after Sawyer and fight a war to regain Wolf City, I was going to have to take trips away from my baby and stop breastfeeding.

"Mommy has to go plan a big escape. Can you stay with Grandma and Auntie Raven a little longer?" I asked Creek.

"Of course!" my mom and Raven said simultaneously.

I looked up at mom. "Mom, how do I...dry out the girls? Assuming we have enough formula in stock?" I pointed to my chest.

She nodded in understanding, cheeks reddening as Rab and Arrow suddenly turned their backs on us to give us privacy.

"We have more than enough, and I know it's a tough decision, but I think given your situation, it might be best. You just stop. It will be painful, and you can hand express to get a little relief, but naturally you will dry up."

My throat tightened in emotion at the thought of just stopping breastfeeding; it had become so natural to me. Definitely freaked me out in the beginning, but then it was this amazing thing that kept my kid alive.

I nodded, kissing Creek's head, and handed him back to her.

"It's best if someone else bottle-feeds him until you dry out so he doesn't smell your milk. Is it okay if I take over the feedings?" my mom asked.

Emotion welled up inside of me, a deep sadness that Creek wouldn't need me as much for survival anymore, but I knew this was for the best given our current situation.

I just nodded. "Thanks, Mom," I croaked. "Thanks, Raven," I added, and pulled my bestie in for a hug.

She squeezed me hard. "I love you, but you smell."

I burst into laughter and pulled back with a smile.

"Please tell me we have hot water here," Sage called out behind me.

Rab nodded. "This way. I'll show you the lavatories."

———·—·———

Thirty minutes later, every square inch of my body had been scrubbed with a yummy-smelling coconut-vanilla soap and I'd shaved off all of my body hair. I scrubbed my scalp so hard it hurt, massaging my hand all the way to the ends with the sudsy soap. The conditioner was heaven; my hair had never felt so smooth.

"Holy crap, that was…" Sage looked at me wide-eyed

with her bright red hair tied up into a damp knot. She was wearing some military-issued black fatigues, same as me, and we stood in the locker room–style shower staring at each other with our newfound cleanness.

"Pretty amazing." I grinned.

Sage smiled, but then her face fell a little. "I mean… not as amazing as hearing the bubbling creek after you stepped out of the shower and looked out onto the thick forest."

We both stared at the concrete walls with dismay.

"No. It's not," I agreed. I would always have a love-hate relationship with the Dark Woods. They made me realize I needed nature but also kept me from those that I loved. We brushed our teeth and flossed, and then stepped out to find Arrow waiting for us.

"Meeting is this way. We've got Rab, Eugene, and then Star. She's the leader of the defector witches. And also Rick. He's the representative of the Independent Society of Werewolves."

I stopped and stared at Arrow with my mouth hung open. "The what?"

That was good that we had some witches in here with us. I was going to need magical help, but Independent Society of Werewolves? What the hell was that?

Arrow sighed. "They formed after Sawyer was taken. They claim to need nor have no leader, nor follow any laws, and just want to exist harmoniously and not take sides with anyone."

I snorted. "That's fucking convenient." This Rick character was about to get his ass handed to him, because I wasn't in the mood for a bunch of freeloaders.

Arrow stopped in front of a large metal door and pulled it open, ushering us inside. Sage and I stepped into the dimly lit room, and I couldn't help but feel like I'd just walked into a coffin. The entire feeling of being underground was suffocating.

The four leaders sat around a metal table, and quieted as I approached.

Eugene and Rab nodded to me in respect and I did so in return. Then I focused on the witch. Her long black hair was dyed purple at the tips, and she was younger than I expected. She looked about my age. Her fingernails were extra long and bright lime green, and she wore a flowing black dress that skimmed the floor.

"Hi, I'm Demi. Alpha of the werewolves." I extended my hand to her.

"Star, leader of the Witches' Revolution." She took my hand and shook it with a firm grasp, which I liked. I also liked that she led the Witches' Revolution.

"Happy to have you here," I told her, then I narrowed my eyes on the giant man who sat with his arms crossed over his chest, making his biceps pop. He was in his late forties and wore a white crisp linen top with some kind of crystal shard around his neck. He smelled of patchouli oil and indecision, and I immediately didn't like him.

"Hi. Rick, is it?" I pinned him with a direct gaze. "I've been informed the Independent Society of Werewolves has no leader and no laws, so you can leave now."

His mouth popped open, and Star, who sat next to him, grinned.

"It's true we don't believe in hierarchy or a chain of command, but I was assured we would be respected in the decision-making process of what happens to this community as a whole." He looked at me like I was a bitch, and for some reason it pleased me.

Leaning forward, pressing both palms to the table, I stared him down. "*This* is a room for leaders. *This* is a room for people who are about to decide how to end a war. This is a room for men and women who make hard decisions that, later, their people will benefit from. *You* are not that person. Go. *Now*."

He stood so fast, his chair skidded backward, the metal scraping against the concrete so loud that it made my skin crawl. I missed the sounds of the birds and the bubbling creek right now.

"This is why we don't want leaders. You're all bullies," he snapped.

He moved to step past me, and I snaked to the right, lining up to block his path so that he was forced to stare me down. "When we leave, you're welcome to come and follow my command and my rules. Or you can stay and see how long the food lasts down here. It's your choice."

He swallowed hard, nervousness crawling into his features, then I stepped aside and he left the room.

It was a bad way to start a new leadership position, but I was inheriting a shitty situation in which I had to act extra hardcore now so I wouldn't be challenged later. After what Rab told me had been going on in my absence, it was necessary. Sawyer wasn't here, so I was going to have to lead two packs and take no shit lest I have complete chaos on my hands.

"Sorry about that," I told everyone left in our group. "I just want to make sure that later on, down the line, everything runs smoothly and there are no freeloaders. It's going to take a lot of work to fit everyone in Paladin Village and live off the land."

Rab nodded and so did Eugene.

"Witches are fine with hard work. We just want sunshine and fresh air," Star said. "How can we help?"

I relaxed, grateful to have her so easily committing to hard work. "Rab, how did you get the thousands of Paladins in here without being seen or smelled? We're going to need to get everyone out. Probably over multiple days, hopefully without anyone knowing until we are all back on Paladin land and in a strong place to protect ourselves."

Rab nodded to Star. "Star and her coven helped. They did a spell that masked scent and sound, and we snuck people in through the hedge in the dead of night."

The hedge was a godsend, but twenty-four thousand

people was a lot. "We have a lot of people to get out, and I'd like to do it over a maximum of two days. I don't think the vampires will care to even go into the Wild Lands. It's the Ithaki we will have to contend with."

Eugene nodded. "I can attest that most of the Magic City territories avoid the Wild Lands. As long as we lie low in Paladin Village, they probably won't even notice we are there."

Sage cleared her throat behind me. I'd totally forgotten she was even here. "Do the vampires know that a bunch of us survived?" she asked.

Great question.

Eugene nodded. "We overheard them saying there weren't enough dead bodies to have gotten all of us. They know we are hiding somewhere."

Rab tipped his head. "And you're sure it's safe to go back? The fungus is gone? We can grow food again? Clean water?"

I smiled, reaching out to squeeze his hand. "I promise." I couldn't explain my experience in the cave if I tried. But I saw the land heal before my eyes, Astra too. "It's time to go home," I assured him.

"I saw it on my way out," Sage piped up behind me again. "Green grass all growing back, fields showed new growth too." Her voice held pride.

Why was she still standing? Did she not think she had permission to sit or something? I pulled out a chair next to me and patted the seat. "Oh, by the way, Sage is my second-in-command. You can bring any concerns you have to her and she'll get them to me."

Rab bristled for a second, maybe thinking I would give the honor to him, but she pulled a baby from my vagina and we'd been through hell together, so it was always going to be her. My ride or die.

"Alright." Rab cleared his throat.

"Fine by me," Star added.

"Welcome to the leaders' table." Eugene winked at her.

I looked up to see her swallow hard, frozen like a deer in headlights. Pulling on her wrist, I yanked her into the seat and carried on.

"The second we get everyone to Paladin Village, I want to build up security first—a huge fence, patrols, and lookouts. That goes before our comforts, understood?"

They all nodded.

"And then when I feel we are settled and safe, I will take Sage and leave to get Sawyer. Leaving you three in charge while I'm gone. Can you handle that?"

Rab puffed up his chest a little at that and they all nodded at the same time.

"Okay..." I cracked my knuckles. "Give me every idea you have on how to get us all out of here in the shortest amount of time without tipping off the vampires. I don't want them knowing how many of us are left. Best to surprise them with that later, when we take back Wolf City."

Over the next hour, everyone shouted out wild ideas while Sage scribbled them down furiously and we tore each one apart for weak points. The witches were low on supplies for spell casting and needed to make a supply run if they were to shroud that many people. We decided that Sage's distraction to get her and Creek inside was actually something brilliant that could be recreated on a larger scale to draw any vampire or fey patrols away from the bunker while we snuck out. We determined even at a brisk pace it would take four hours to move twenty-four thousand people, and that's with everyone packed and having practiced a dry run and being fully prepared.

"How do you draw someone away for over four hours…" I mused aloud. My eyes fell to the cuffs on my wrist, and then it came to me.

"They still want me," I breathed, tracing my finger over the cuff. "What if I lead them on a wild-goose chase?"

"Too dangerous," Rab inserted.

"No way!" Sage yelled.

"You could be caught," Eugene piped in.

Star was silent, and I looked at her.

"Aren't you like super vampire fast and can walk through walls and stuff?" She looked at the cuffs on my wrists and I smiled. The rumor mill had gone around even in my absence.

"My wolf can walk through walls yes, and I *am* very fast."

Star shrugged. "I mean if you can outrun a vampire, then I think it's safe to say you have a great chance of not getting caught."

She was so right. Everyone here was trying to protect me, which I admired, but what the hell was I afraid of? If I took off the cuffs and let the vamps scent me, then I could lead them on a chase while everyone got out. Then I would just put the cuffs back on when I wanted to hide again.

"What if we could get everyone out in one night? I could take off the cuffs, lead them away from the Wild Lands, and then put them back on and meet up with you."

"Run for four hours straight! That's too long. You'll collapse from exhaustion."

He was probably right, but wasn't that what marathoners did?

"I could take them off and on as I needed breaks. I hiked the mountain in the Dark Woods every day for nearly a year. I'm in the best shape of my life. I can do this."

"And she can control bears!" Sage blurted out, and every person at the table's eyes went wide.

"I'm not sure how useful that will be in the city." I laughed.

Sage shook her head. "No. What I mean is…I think you used…compulsion. I think you could do it again on a lower-level vampire to confuse them."

Compulsion was a myth, right? But in that moment, I was reminded of the piece of paper Sawyer tore out of that book that explained split shifters. Didn't it say they could do compulsion?

Star leaned forward, eyes wide. "You can compel?"

I squirmed in my seat. "I mean, I did once to a bear, maybe twice, but..."

Everyone was staring at me like I was an alien.

Eugene looked intrigued. "It wouldn't work on the queen or those high up in her coven, but a lower-level vampire for sure."

That was good to know.

"So we're doing this?" I asked. "One night? Get everyone out and then I'll meet you back at Paladin Village when I know it's safe?"

Everyone regarded each other, eyes darting around the room to find someone to disagree with.

"We can't stay down here much longer...and getting out into the open air, building a community together, it would be good for morale," Eugene said.

"Then it's settled!" I smacked my open palm on the table.

"Hold up." Rab put his fingers out in a gesture of calm. "And what's the plan if we get caught and war breaks out again?"

He was right. We needed a fallback plan for that. "Eugene, do we still have a good weapons cache?"

He nodded. "The base level is full of them."

"Any grenades?" I raised one eyebrow, and he nodded with a smile.

"Okay, if we get caught, you run east toward the Witch Lands and we funnel them into the Wild Lands at the border. There, we will set off the grenades as a distraction, before doubling back and going back into hiding," I told them.

"Genius." Rab sat up. "I can set the traps tonight with Arrow. When are we doing this?"

I wanted to get to Sawyer as soon as possible. "Tomorrow night. Start preparing everyone now. One bag for each person, only what they can carry, and they will line up in alphabetical order of family last name. Do a trial run on the morning of the lineup."

"I'll sneak out with Rab and Arrow later tonight with one of my witches and get the spell supplies needed," Star added.

We had a plan. My first real day as alpha and I didn't completely screw it up.

I looked at Rab. "Where is medical? I need to check on Astra."

I needed to make sure my number one fan was okay.

———•·•———

Astra was lying in the fetal position on a cot in the medical ward, fast asleep. I'd spoken to the doctor who treated her, a nice submissive wolf in his late fifties. He said he'd given her IV fluids and a feeding tube for the time being, but he was confident he could take it out by morning. He just wanted to load her up with nutrients, and she was too weak to chew and swallow right now. My heart twisted in agony as I saw bones protruding from her back in her thin hospital gown. This young girl had been through hell for me, and it was important to me to take care of her from now on.

"Alpha," she croaked, and I scrambled to the other side of her bed where I could face her. She looked up at me with heavy eyes. The doctor said he'd given her some pain medication to ease the discomfort of the feeding tube while her shifter healing kicked in.

"Astra." I fell to my knees before her and took her small hands in mine. "I just wanted to check on you. I'm getting us out of here, back to Paladin Village, and everything is going to be okay."

"I heard you in your despair," she said softly, eyes closing in exhaustion. I frowned, confused.

"What?"

She blinked a few times as if her eyelids were too heavy to hold up. "In the Dark Woods, when you were at your lowest point and you cried out to God. I heard it."

Chills raced up my spine. I didn't know if she was being serious or just high as a kite. But there was one night, on my third day there, before I found the cabin, that I was starving, thirsty, and helpless, and I'd screamed at the sky, aiming my desperation at the man upstairs.

"I knew you would come back. I knew you would make it. And now everything is going to be fine." She smiled, her eyes rolling closed as she fell asleep, the steady rise and fall of her chest making me sleepy as well.

I wondered what it was like to live with that much blind faith in something. I wasn't capable of it, but she clearly was. Faith in me, in God, in everything. This small thing had more faith than our entire pack combined, and I wasn't going to let her down.

Leaning forward, I placed a kiss on her cheek and made a promise to make the world a safer and better place for people like Astra.

———·•——

Sleeping next to little Creek, all snuggled in a soft bed with real blankets and pillows, was heaven. Sage slept above us on the top bunk of a shared room. Rab said he could arrange for me to have some fancy captain's quarters and kick a family out that was sharing it, but I insisted I be treated like everyone else. It was only for one night anyway, and I didn't think Sage and I were ready to live separate lives just yet. We hadn't said it out loud, but we'd both become each other's support and comfort person over our time in the Dark Woods. Coming back to reality was nice, but also a shock. We needed to ease into it.

Creek nursed once in the night, but my mom came and took him in the morning to bottle-feed him, and after a large breakfast, we went over the drill with the entire bunker. We had them all line up in alphabetical order based on family last name.

And…it was a total shit show.

Rab had drawn letters on paper, *A* through *Z*, and taped them along the hallways, but we'd underestimated how many of each letter there were and people with *A* last names were lined up all the way into *C*, which meant *C* was pushing to move up. It didn't go well, but we'd adjusted where the letters were, and I had faith that tonight it would work. It had to.

"Knock, knock," Raven called into the war room as I peered up from the Wolf City maps I was looking at.

I grinned at the sight of my bestie. We'd had no time to catch up, and yet a friendship this old and close made it feel like not even a day had gone by since we'd last talked.

"Hey." I waved her in and she gave me a quick hug before settling next to me and looking at the maps.

"I heard about your plan to lead the vampires on a chase and I came up with an idea." She pulled out a small baggy of tiny plastic cap–looking things.

"What are those?" I inspected them.

She pulled out a cap and broke off the top to reveal a thin, barely visible needle. "Needles usually made to test blood sugar. We use them in spell work when we need only a tiny drop of blood."

217

Modern day witch tools. I guess it beat cutting your palm open like in the movies.

"I was thinking...in order to get the vampires to scent you and follow a coordinated trail, you could prick your finger with the cuffs off and leave blood somewhere. Then run away from that place and put the cuffs back on. Then repeat this for a few hours until Rab signals that we are all out."

I grinned. "Raven, that's genius!"

The blood would be like vampire candy and make it stronger and easier for them to scent me, allowing me to bring them exactly where I wanted them.

She pulled her nails up to her mouth and huffed on them, before buffing them off on her shoulder. "I mean, no biggie." She winked.

Reaching out, I took her hand in mine. "You've been such a good friend. It's hard to believe over a year ago we were going to Delphi, and now..."

She nodded, squeezing my hand. "I know."

We sat there for a moment in the dimly lit and quiet room until finally she stood. "I gotta pack my bag. Excited to get out of here and back into nature." She looked around at the concrete walls.

I nodded and she turned to leave.

"Hey, Raven?"

She spun to face me.

"I know I've been gone and we haven't had much time to catch up, but..." My voice cracked.

She grinned and tears lined her eyes. "Love you too, babe."

I chuckled. She always knew what I was going to say.

She left the room, and I tucked the finger pokers into my pocket. I was going to pack a small bag of protein bars and water and then get ready for my night of running.

Of being prey.

CHAPTER THIRTEEN

I ZOOMED THROUGH THE WOODS AT THE NORTH SIDE of Wolf City before taking a break to lean against a tree, panting from the exertion. I'd pricked my fingers raw, dapping little dots of blood on trees, or doors of houses or car windows. Then they would heal up and I'd throw on my cuffs before zooming off. It had worked, but now the city was crawling with vampires. They'd pulled everyone from Sterling Hill and the surrounding area and put them on the hunt for me. When my cuffs were on, they couldn't scent me, not like they normally would. I probably smelled human. I was able to hide behind buildings and catch parts of their conversations. The queen had been called in when they recognized it as my blood, and they all thought I was injured, which was good.

I'd been at this for two hours and I'd already had

to kill two of them because they were catching up with me. I was slowing down, getting weaker. I shoved half a hunk of protein bar in my mouth to keep my energy up and mentally checked in with Rab while I chewed.

'How's it going?'

'Good, we've got half our people out. There was a bit of a close call with a scout in the woods, but we killed him before he could report back. The first wave of people have reached Paladin Village. Your parents, Astra, and the baby are with them.'

That was a huge relief. 'Okay, thanks. Check in the moment you're all out, or if something goes wrong.'

'Will do.'

I heard the snapping of a tree branch and ripped off the cuffs before taking off into the woods. The issue with wearing the cuffs was that I was basically human with them on, which was good for masking smell but bad for fighting or running fast. I could only outrun the vamps with them off, which led them to my general location eventually.

I can do this...just another hour or so, I thought as my muscles burned and strained to keep up with my superhuman movement. I was just heading west to cut across the stretch of woods that lay in that direction when I felt him.

Sawyer. His presence filled me up so strongly, so quickly, that I gasped, and an involuntary sob escaped me.

'My love,' his voice boomed inside my head. 'I feel

*you for the first time in a year. I only have seconds. Tell
me you're alive and well.'*

I burst into tears at the sudden adoration and
completeness that filled me up at his words. *'I'm alive.
I...'* How did you tell someone you had a secret baby in
the woods they didn't know about?

You just did it...

*'I was pregnant before I left and didn't know. We
have a baby boy, Creek Curt Calloway-Hudson.'*

Shock ripped through our bond as his feelings filtered
into me for the first time in a year, and then a surge of
joy and pride followed. *'Demi. A boy. That's amazing,
you're amazing. I...'*

He was silent, speechless as I would expect.

'I'm coming to get you,' I said. *'I just need a few
days to get everyone situated from the bunker to the
Paladin Village, and then I'm coming.'*

Panic seized our bond. *'No, don't. That's what they
want, they're wait—'*

His voice cut off, as did his presence, and I was left
with such a sudden empty feeling it made me physically
sick. I slowed my run, slapping the cuffs on as I burst
into a puddle of tears. I continued to jog at human speed,
but my mind raced frantically.

They're waiting for me? To come get him? Is
that what he was going to say before he was cut off?
Whatever magic they did over our bond must have its
limits because he'd been able to push through for a short

moment. Which meant that maybe he could do it again now that he knew I was back. What if he'd been trying every few days for the past year? The thought shook me. There was no way I wasn't going to bust him out of there. But if they were waiting for me to do that, I was more hesitant. I needed a plan. I needed to know more about Magic City Prison before I just went barging in there, right?

I chewed on my lip, my mind engrossed in thoughts of Sawyer and rescuing him, and kissing him, and his wonderful reaction to our son, when I felt the air whoosh past me. Reaching out, I tried to rip the cuff off so I could run super fast, when a hand clamped over mine to stop me. The fingernails were painted red, and I *knew* I was about to look up into the eyes of the vampire queen.

"Oh, you have no idea how glad I am to know that you are still alive," she purred as someone came up and grabbed me from behind. Strong arms yanked my hands behind me and held them tightly against my back, so tightly that I whimpered in pain.

Shit.

'Rab, I've been caught. Plan B,' I told him. We'd been delighted to learn that with these cuffs I could still mentally speak.

'On it,' he responded immediately.

We had decided that should I be caught, we would still go ahead and set off the grenades and create the diversion to hopefully buy me time to get away.

I yanked my arm quickly out of the grasp of the person who stood behind me and my wrist slipped free of the cuff.

"Hold her by the shoulders," the queen snapped, her eyes going fully black. "I need these cuffs off to siphon her power." The iron viselike grip shifted to my shoulder and tightened. That's when my fight-or-flight kicked in. I started to buck like a wild woman against the man who held me. Nothing like the word *siphon* to really set you off.

Pulling out a sleek black gun, the queen held it to the side of my temple and I froze, going completely still.

Fuck.

There were many things I felt confident outrunning or fighting against. A gun to the head was not one of them.

'Now would be a great time for plan B,' I reiterated to Rab. Maybe with the distraction, I could get away from them and not get siphoned or my head blown off.

'Slight issue. Almost there,' he called back.

Great.

Queen Drake's hair was pulled into such a tight bun that it lifted the edge of her eyes in a catlike way. "I need to sample the goods, dear," she purred as her teeth extended, pressing into her bottom lip. "I want to see what all the fuss is about. Something I should have done before." She reached up with her free hand, and grasped the sides of my face, just as her minion yanked my other cuff off. It fell with a thud to the forest floor.

I couldn't see the dude holding me from behind, but I could tell by the strong grip that he was powerful. His fingernails dug painfully into my shoulders while she held the gun to my head.

There was literally no way out of this for me. My wolf rattled my skin in an effort to break free but I kept her down. I didn't fancy leaving my son without a mother.

A buzzing vibration started to radiate from her fingertips. The same buzz I'd felt when I'd shaken the prime minister's hand. That must be how they sensed my power or something.

"Oh yes," she hummed, and brought her lips closer to mine.

I recoiled the tiniest bit, unsure if she was going to kiss me or bite me or what. That's when the white light started to leak from my skin. She breathed in, and it funneled into her mouth, her eyes lighting up the same deep blue hue as mine, which made her look even more crazed than she already did. How the hell had breathing in my power changed her freaking eye color!?

Before I could dwell on that, pain laced up my spine as I felt her *feeding* off of my essence. I bucked a little, but then she pushed the gun harder into my head.

"Now, let's see if your blood is even more potent." She grinned like a lunatic, and the next second her teeth sank into my neck. I gasped as pleasure and pain slammed into me with equal measure. The tips of vampire teeth had some type of mild narcotic on them that made you crave their bite. It was psychologically fucking with me to have her feeding off my neck and have it feel good.

"No..." I whimpered.

What happened if she fully drained my essence? Would I die? Or would I just no longer have these extra powers? I had a son to live for now, I had to get out of this situation *fast*, but I couldn't make any sudden movements, or she'd blow my head off.

'Would she really? She needs you,' my wolf said.

My wolf was right. She wanted my power juice, she wasn't going to shoot me...right?

'Boom time in three,' Rab's voice called out through our bond and I steeled myself. Just in the nick of time. *'Two...one...'* An explosion rocked the eastern border of our land. The queen jerked her head back in shock as her eyelids fluttered open. Crimson blood stained her lips as she glanced over her shoulder to look at what had caused such a great noise.

It was go time.

Striking out with my thumb, I rammed it into the armpit of her hand holding the gun to my head, and that arm collapsed to her side. Then I butted my head backward and was met with a satisfying crunch and a yelp. Wasting no time, I twisted out of his hold and crouched to the ground where my cuffs lay. Snatching them up, I burst out from between the queen's legs, knocking her over with a yelp of surprise. Then I ran faster than I ever had in my life, still a bit cloudy from the effects of the bite. I had just broken through the thicket of trees when I felt an unseen force slam into me and knock me to the ground.

What the...?

Tripping over my feet, I fumbled and tucked my head in as I did a full somersault. Pain exploded in my shoulder, but I ignored it and popped up quickly. The queen cackled somewhere behind me.

"Oh, this feels good!" she shrieked with glee.

Dread sank into my gut like a heavy stone. She was using *my* own powers against me. On instinct, I pulled out the silver stake I'd placed in my waistband earlier and chucked it about ten feet off to the side. If she wanted to play this game, I was going to play. Hadn't Sawyer said when he'd kissed me the first time and accidently taken my power that he'd been able to run really fast but it wore off quickly? I could only hope that was the case here because, at this rate, I wasn't going to be able to get back to Paladin Village without her trailing me.

I stood just as she skidded to a stop before me. "Oh, my darling," she purred. "You are *delicious* and worth every inconvenience. Now, be a good girl and come with me so we can harvest a plasma serum from your essence. After that, you are free to go. You have my word."

Plasma serum.

"Plasma serum for what?" I asked. Curiosity killed the cat. And the wolf too.

"To permanently enhance my people with your abilities of course." She rubbed her hands together in greed.

Oh hell no. I wasn't a fucking lab experiment.

"Enhance this, bitch."

The entire time she'd been standing there, I'd been wrapping my power around the silver stake on the ground like a force field, slowly raising it into the air. Now at my will, it shot forward and slammed into her torso from behind. The stake popped out the other side of her chest, bringing with it a sludge of black blood. Her eyes widened; she yelped in shock. It wasn't a direct kill hit, more near the armpit, but it would buy me time.

I spun, snaking through the trees. My heart beat so loudly I could hear it in my brain. It felt like a drum pumping throughout my entire body. Crossing the grasslands, leaping over farm fences, I finally jumped into a barn, skidding to a stop inches from a cow, and slipped my cuffs on so that I hopefully couldn't be scented.

The cow mooed and I nodded to him. "Hey, buddy. Mind if I hide out here awhile?"

His tail swished, but he turned away from me, unconcerned with my presence. If I could lie low here for an hour to make sure I wasn't followed, then it might be safe enough to head back to Paladin Village. Assuming everyone was out. Reaching up, I traced the two small divots in my neck, already healing, only a slight scar there that would be gone in an hour. A shiver ran through me at the memory of her sucking on my blood.

I quickly checked my body for cuts, or blood, or any abrasion that might lead the vampires to sniff me out, even with my cuffs on, when my gaze fell onto the giant cow dung patty that lay on the floor.

The pungent odor was vile, but also strong enough to mask everything else.

Sometimes survival was gross, but I was going to have to do what it took to stay alive and lie low. Grabbing a handful of cow dung, I rubbed it onto the front of my black army fatigues, gagging through the process. I rubbed two strips along the front of my legs, and two along my arms, before backing away from the dung in an effort to escape the smell. Except I couldn't...now I *was* the smell.

Gross. I fought down a gag as I scanned the space for a place to lie low. I spied a tack room in the corner, with a sink inside, and ran in to wash my hands with soap. On the far wall, hanging near some saddles and helmets, was a handkerchief.

Thank God.

Using my clean hands, I wrapped the hanky around my nose and mouth, breathing a sigh of relief that the smell had lessened to a manageable amount.

'*You okay? Did it work?*' Rab asked suddenly.

'*I got free. Hiding out now in a barn. Will wait an hour and then meet you. Everyone get out?*'

I felt his relief through our bond. '*Everyone but the Independent Council of Douchebags. They decided to stay.*'

I almost growled, but in case the queen and her men were stalking around the barn, I didn't want to call attention to myself with noise. '*Well, it's their funeral. I don't care,*' I said grumpily.

But I did care. I wanted all of us together. I didn't want Sawyer to come out of prison only to see his people broken into multiple groups, but I couldn't control them, so whatever.

'*All okay at the village?*'

'*We had to take care of a few Ithaki on the outskirts, but I'm heading there now. Arrow went with the first group. He says it's deserted and completely fertile for planting crops. Fully restored. Good job, Alpha.*'

I grinned, taking pride in his praise. It might have taken me a year to restore that damn land, but I restored it and that's all that mattered. I settled into the tack room, sitting in a corner and staying out of sight, expecting at any moment that the vampires could track my scent, but they never came. Maybe I'd injured the queen worse than I thought. Maybe she was in need of some lifesaving surgery or something. That would be awesome.

I was so tired that my thigh muscles quivered even though I was sitting. I'd run too long and hard and my body was hurting. The minutes ticked by agonizingly slow, and my eyelids started to droop.

No.

I couldn't fall asleep here. That would be a death sentence. Popping up, I paced the room to stay awake, trying to ignore the exhaustion pulling at my limbs. I'd run nonstop for hours, then the queen stole some of my essence. It was a wonder I was still conscious.

After a while, I decided it was now or never. Time to head to Paladin Village.

I tiptoed out into the main barn, seeing that the door was still ajar, just as I'd left it. I would keep the cuffs on and have to just rely on my normal human jogging speed to get back to the village, because I wasn't going to risk spreading my scent around for the vampires.

Slipping out of the barn, I crossed the farmland, and quickly tucked into the trees that bordered the Wild Lands. I knew on the other side was the Ithaki portion, but I had no choice. I'd rather brave them than the vampires right now. Stepping over the orange flags that demarcated the property line, I started a brisk jog through the woods.

'*On my way,*' I told Rab. '*If I don't run into trouble, I should reach you in the next thirty minutes.*'

'*I see you. Go right,*' he said, and shock caused me to slow and look around.

"What?" I whispered out loud.

Rab, Sage, Arrow, and Eugene stepped out from behind an outcrop of trees. They were armed to the teeth and covered in mud paint to camouflage themselves.

"You didn't think we were going to leave you on your own, did you?" Sage winked.

My throat tightened at the sight of my little protection

231

squad. Their loyalty made tears form in my eyes as I swallowed hard. One by one, their noses wrinkled as they took in the stench covering me.

"No offense, Alpha," Arrow said, "but you smell like shit."

Sage pinched her nose. "Literal shit."

I grinned. "Cow dung. Threw off the vampires. Come on, let's get home so I can shower."

With that, we crept through the woods together, working as one unit. I was so used to doing things on my own and having no one else to rely on except for Sage, that I'd forgotten what this felt like. This feeling of being cared for and looked after.

———•—

We encountered no trouble on our way back to the Paladin village, and I was pleased to see the wall around the city being repaired, city and Paladin wolves working side by side, building it higher than ever before.

"They'll work all night on the fence and only sleep when it's complete," Rab told me.

"And the witches said they can do repellent charms and magical trip-wire alarms to alert us of an attack," Sage added.

"Awesome," I breathed.

Because I was going to need to sleep about twenty-four hours after this marathon of a night, and I would sleep more soundly with a twelve-foot wall around my home and magic repellent charms. Once we stepped inside the village, there was a flurry of activity. People were erecting temporary tents in the middle of the open road. Homes were being swept out with corn husk brooms and repaired. The meeting hall was being rebuilt, with people already laying bricks. It was like the second people saw a place they could live, they threw everything they had into making it a home. Children were running through the streets, weaving in and out of the tents and pointing up at the darkened sky.

"It's the moon, it's the moon!" they yelled.

"Bonus of having over twenty thousand wolves," Rab stated. "We'll have the city restored in no time."

"What's the food situation?" I asked him as we walked to the birthing center, which was doubling as our medical ward. I spied Astra through the open door, sitting up and drinking something warm.

"Willow buried a giant tin capsule of thousands of seeds before we left. They are still there. We will sow them tomorrow indoors until the weather is better to transplant them outside. Until then, we will hunt and fish."

I nodded, no longer afraid to be without food as I would have been before my year in the Dark Woods. I lived day-to-day out there, trusting that nature would bring me my next meal, and she always did.

"The creek behind the cornfields is full of salmon,"

Arrow piped in. "And the walnut and citrus groves were fully restored when you healed the land. I'll do inventory of the other permanent crops, but I imagine it will be the same."

That was the best news ever. I nodded and breathed a sigh of relief. Now that I was alpha, I could *feel* our land. I knew how big it was, where the borders were, and all the streams and waterways. It was so large that we had only populated twenty percent of it. The rest was left wild and natural, which would be perfect for hunting.

"Sage." I turned to my bestie and new second-in-command. "Get a team of hunters together, go after big game."

After our time in the woods together, Sage and I were masters at catching a meal. Starvation turns you into an expert quickly.

She nodded. "You got it." Then she scurried off.

"Rab can you figure out who will be best on security detail? I want this place crawling with armed wolves. We will not be taken unaware again."

He bowed slightly to me. "Yes, Alpha."

'*My love.*' Sawyer's voice invaded my head and my breath caught in my throat. '*Things are not looking good here... This might be the last time we speak and I just wanted you to know that I love you so much, and if I can't make it back to you, I want you to lead our people and raise our son and just be happy, okay?*'

Our people. Last time we speak?

My heart hammered in my chest. *'What do you mean? Why are you saying that?'*

'Sometimes we have to know when to quit. Didn't you tell me that?' He sounded dejected, like he'd lost all hope. Something must have happened, something bad.

I did say that, dammit, but I wasn't ready to give up.

'No, I'm not giving up on this, on us. There is no happiness without you, Sawyer.'

'It's too late, my love.' His voice faded and I knew I was losing him.

Desperation rushed through me. *'Don't say that! Don't lose hope. I can walk through fucking walls Sawyer, I—'*

'Not here love.'

My heart fell in my chest. *'I'll find a way. We'll be a family. No one tells me what I can and can't do.'* I growled at him.

'God I miss that smart fucking mouth. I miss the way you taste.' Sawyer moaned and a tear slipped free from the corner of my eyes, rolling down my cheek.

'Sawyer, I will get you out. I'll think of something brilliant and I'll get you out.'

'I gotta go. I love you so much,' he said. I felt him leaving as panic seized me.

'I'm leaving right now. Just hold on. I'll be there in a few days!' I frantically thought through scenarios of how I could get into Light Fey Territory undetected. Tears slid

down my face, and I was about to speak again, when a female wail cut through the night. It sounded familiar, but I couldn't put my finger on who it was. Then she screamed again and I recognized it as Sawyer's mother.

Oh God.

A stone sank in my stomach as I took off running in the direction of the scream, with Rab and Eugene hot on my trail. It sucked to run at human speeds after knowing what I was capable of, but it was the only way to cover my scent. I had to wear these damn cuffs.

Crisscrossing through the tents and children and general chaos of twenty thousand displaced people with duffel bags, I finally found her. She was in my cottage, the guesthouse I'd stayed in when I lived here for a short while, sitting in the dusty living room clutching a hand crank radio that my dad was pumping to keep on. My mom stared at the radio in shock while she held baby Creek to her chest.

"What happened?" I asked, but the man on radio started to speak and I froze, listening intently.

"So that's the latest news from Light Fey City. Just to recap, Sawyer Hudson, former alpha of Wolf City, has been sentenced to death for his crimes and will be executed via guillotine one week from today."

A strangled howl cut through my throat as the room spun around me.

Sawyer...death sentence. *Executed.* Did they change his sentence? So suddenly? Did Queen Drake have anything to do with it? Maybe my running off had inspired her to put in a call. I couldn't process it all, and before I knew it, black dots danced at the edges of my vision. I started to fall backward, but before I hit the ground, a pair of giant arms caught me, and then Eugene's voice was there.

"It's okay. I got you."

The day had been too hard. I'd run too long, this news was too dark. Instead of fighting the blackness pressing at the edges of my vision, I gave in. A person could only be so strong before they broke, and I'd reached my breaking point.

———•—•—

I came to and immediately reached for the baby, only to find that he wasn't next to me. Everything came back to me in a rush, and I gasped in panic, until I heard my mother's voice.

"Shh, I got him, don't worry," she whispered from the dark corner of the room, where she sat in a chair, bottle-feeding him.

I lay back on the bed, letting my heart slow. The first shafts of light of a new day were bleeding into the room, highlighting the dust slowly settling in the air.

Sawyer. They were going to murder the love of my life, and I just couldn't live with myself if I sat back and did nothing, no matter the cost.

I sat up. "Mom...I have to get Sawyer out of there." I ran my fingers through my tangled hair, glad to find someone had changed my cow dung clothes, probably my mother. But I still wanted a shower desperately.

My mom stood, bringing Creek with her as she sat at the edge of the bed. He played with a loose strand of her golden blond hair and it made me smile to see the bond they were forming.

"Honey, listen to me and listen carefully." My mom's voice was firm and strong, and when I met her gaze I saw a fierceness there. "I used to worry *so much* about you. Especially after your attack. But even just going to Sterling Hill, I worried you would be hurt, killed, heartbroken, all of the things every parent worries about."

I reached out and patted her free hand, totally understanding now that I had a child of my own.

"But I don't worry anymore," she said matter-of-factly. "Something about being gone in those woods has changed you. You're more capable now than ever. I pity the person who gets in the way of you bringing Sawyer home. You can do *anything*, Demi. I see that now."

Her words knocked the breath out of me, lighting a fire inside of me that had gone out last night when I'd heard the bad news. She was right. *No one* was taking Sawyer from me, not before he got to meet his son and not before I got to love him at least eighty more years.

I stood, looking down at her and the baby, reaching out to stroke Creek's head as he cooed.

I nodded to my mom. "You'll watch him? Make sure he's safe?"

My mom snuggled Creek to her chest. "With my very last breath."

Leaving him would be hard, but I had to do this. I couldn't live in a world where I sat idly by as Sawyer was killed for fixing a mistake the justice system made.

I nodded to my mother, and then leaned down to kiss Creek's forehead. He looked at me with those deep blue eyes and I made my son a promise. A promise I intended to keep.

"Mommy's going to get Daddy," I said, and the promise cemented into my heart and worked its way into my bones.

The Dark Woods had turned me into a wild woman, and Magic City Prison was about to suffer my wrath.

SEE HOW DEMI'S STORY WRAPS UP IN

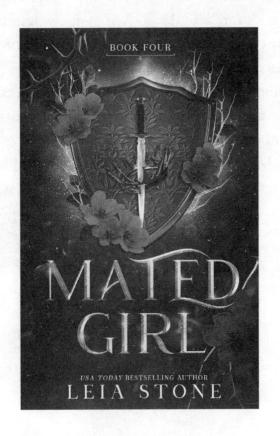

CHAPTER ONE

AFTER TALKING TO MY MOM ABOUT DECIDING TO break Sawyer out of Magic City Prison, I slipped into the shower. The water ran down my body in warm rivulets and I sighed. I was glad that the Ithaki hadn't damaged the gravity-fed water tower when they'd ransacked Paladin Village. I'd missed this, showering with soap and shaving my legs, but I'd be lying if I said I didn't miss that little cabin in the woods and my time there.

My thoughts were a frantic tangle of how exactly I would get to Magic City Prison, which was in the middle of high-tech Light Fey City, and then how I would break Sawyer out. Sawyer had indicated that the vampires would be waiting for me to rescue him, which meant going there was a trap...but I had no way around that. I was a one-woman show, although I knew Sage would insist on going with me and I wouldn't have it any other way…but still. How did two women break into a magic prison? I had seven days to get him out before they killed him, and that was not enough time, especially considering I was basically a wanted woman with a target on my own back.

I forced down the sob that threatened to come back up. Now was not the time for a breakdown. Sawyer had seemed so hopeless when we'd last spoken. It broke my heart. I'd be hopeless too if I'd just been sentenced to death by guillotine.

I couldn't let that happen.

I was also worried about leaving Creek, but if you had to leave your baby with anyone for an extended period of time, it felt good when it was your own mother.

After turning off the tap and changing into fresh clothes, I slipped into the living room to find Eugene, Sage, and Rab all bent over a map of Magic City. They held steaming cups of tea and coffee and were speaking animatedly about something.

"What's going on here?" I asked, frowning at the food wrappers and old coffee cups that littered the table. "Have any of you slept?"

Sage looked like a zombie, hair in a messy bun, dark circles under her eyes, her left foot tapping out a rhythm like she'd had too much coffee.

She grinned as I approached, her eyes widening, which made her look even more amped up. "Eugene knows a guy who broke out of Magic City Prison a decade ago."

I froze, my heart picking up speed until it was a steady thump in my chest. "I...I need to see him. Who is it? I need him to tell me everything, I need—"

"He's a troll," Eugene said, putting up his hands. "Went into hiding years ago. Haven't spoken to him in a decade."

Shit!

I'd assumed a wolf friend, preferably one still alive and here in Paladin Village. I started to pace the room, my mind spinning as I chewed on this new information.

Rab stood, stepping in front of me. "We've been up all night. We've decided that we three will go and try to bring Sawyer back...while you stay and take care of the pack."

I looked at Rab with what I hoped was a grateful expression and not one of murder, which was what I was currently feeling. "That's really sweet, you guys, but I can't let you all do that. I have to be the one to go."

Sawyer was my fucking husband, mate, and baby daddy. No one was going for him but me.

Rab shook his head. "You are the alpha, the most important—"

"What if it was Willow?" I stopped him. "Would you trust anyone else to get her back?"

He sighed, shrugging as a defeated expression crossed his face. "You can't go alone, and we can't leave the entire pack without leadership."

I nodded. "You, Eugene, and Star will lead the pack while Sage and I go. It's been the two of us forever. We can do this together."

I looked at my bestie as her face pinched, like she was fighting the urge to cry.

"I'm totally going, not even up for discussion," she added to Rab.

He growled lightly, running his fingers over the long scar on his face. "We just got an alpha, we are just starting to rebuild…"

I nodded. "And when I bring Sawyer back, we will build back stronger than ever before."

He sighed, giving me a curt nod. Then an idea struck me.

Troll.

The guy Eugene knew was a troll.

"Marmal!" I shouted, causing everyone to jump. "We can go see my troll friend Marmal. Maybe she can help us find this guy that Eugene knows!"

Eugene shrugged from his place on the couch, where he nursed a steaming hot mug. "The trolls are notorious for their gossip and stories. Maybe she's heard of him."

I'm sure she had. Marmal said people in Troll Village paid in gossip. If a fellow troll had escaped Magic City Prison, she would know the story and possibly where to find him.

"We'll leave right away!" I started to look around the room for what to bring.

"Hold up." Rab put his hands out. "Our people *just* settled here. They will want to see you first, to have faith in this new home you've brought them to."

I growled, not excited to play politics right now. But he was right. I'd need to make a small appearance before I left. "Fine. Sage, you get two horses ready. Pack them up with enough food for a week and I'll go make one round outside through the village. We leave in an hour for Troll Village."

I wasn't letting Sawyer die because I had to uphold some image.

Sage nodded and stepped toward me, pulling something from her pocket. "In all the drama, I forgot to give this back. Your mom held on to it for me when I went looking for you." She reached out her hand and my breath caught in my throat.

My ring.

I plucked it from her palm and slipped it on my ring finger. It felt so foreign to wear jewelry after a year in the wild, and yet this ring felt like home. It made me miss Sawyer so much more. "Thank you," I croaked.

ACKNOWLEDGMENTS

A huge thank-you to my editors at Bloom. Christa, Gretchen, and Kylie, you made this baby shine! And to my agents, Flavia and Meire, for always believing in my work. It truly takes a village to get every single book into readers' hands. I have to send out a huge thank-you to my readers for buying my books and turning this passion into a career that supports my family. I'm literally living my dream. Thank you to my amazing and supportive family for sharing me with my characters. And lastly, thank you to God for this truly remarkable gift you have given me.

ABOUT THE AUTHOR

Leia Stone is the *USA Today* bestselling author of multiple bestselling series, including Matefinder, Wolf Girl, The Gilded City, Fallen Academy, and Kings of Avalier. She's sold over three million books, and her Fallen Academy series has been optioned for film. Her novels have been translated into multiple languages and she even dabbles in script writing.

Leia writes urban fantasy and paranormal romance with sassy kick-butt heroines and irresistible love interests. She lives in Spokane, Washington, with her husband and two children.

Instagram: @leiastoneauthor
TikTok: @leiastone
Facebook: leia.stone
Website: www.LeiaStone.com